SLOW MOVING DREAMS

SLOW MOVING DREAMS

A Novel

Tom Hardy

TCU Press

Fort Worth, Texas

Library of Congress Cataloging-in-Publication Data

Hardy, Tom (Tom J.)
Slow moving dreams / by Tom Hardy.
p. cm.
ISBN 978-0-87565-424-9 (pbk.)
1. Texas--Fiction. I. Title.
PS3558.A624S56 2011
813'.54--dc22

2011006100

TCU Press
P. O. Box 298300
Fort Worth, Texas 76129
817.257.7822
http://www.prs.tcu.edu

To order books: 800.826.8911
Designed by Joshua Berman Design

For

Courtney & Allison

"My heroes have always been cowboys,
And they still are it seems.
Always in search of,
And one step in back of
Themselves and their slow moving dreams."

Willie Nelson

Table of Contents

Acknowledgments

I'd like to thank the following friends, associates, and institutions for their help and assistance during the writing of this novel: Gary Rolls, Susan Grant, Ken McAllister, Judy Krohn, Norman Cosper, and Kim Worley. Their willingness to read multiple drafts, provide constructive comments, inspiration, and guidance was invaluable. My gratitude knows no bounds.

I want to thank everyone at TCU Press who made this work possible, especially Judy Alter, Susan Petty, and Katie George. I want to thank Sul Ross State University for allowing me access to their library for research.

While I read many books and articles while researching *Slow Moving Dreams*, I'd like to especially mention *Alpine, Texas, then and now* by Dr. Clifford B. Casey; *Mirages, Mysteries and Reality: Brewster County, Texas, the Big Bend of the Rio Grande* by Dr. Clifford B. Casey; *Texas, a Geography* by Terry G. Jordan with John L. Bean Jr. and William M. Holmes; and *Roadside Geology of Texas* by Darwin Spearing.

Chapter 1

There were three men and a boy in the car, cruising just below posted speed limits on a long, straight, almost flat highway in the Texas Panhandle country on a cold, overcast, blustery day. Winter had not fully taken hold yet, but it was always windy in this flat country, and the wind made it seem colder. During particularly strong gusts they could hear grains of sand speckling the side of the car. They had begun their trip well before dawn, and it was now late afternoon. All four were tired, but they had taken turns with the driving, and there was a nervous energy in all of them. None of those not driving had napped. The purpose of the trip weighed heavily on each of them.

The men all looked to be in their forties, the boy in his younger teens. They wore blue-collar work clothes—khaki pants or jeans and cotton shirts. All four wore the style of lace-up boots that could have been work footwear, or hiking and hunting footgear. The driver, Tom, was a very thin man with sharp, Indian-like features. He had very black hair. The man riding in the front was a heavier man but resembled the driver in facial features. His hair had begun to turn gray though, and he wore wire-rimmed glasses with bifocal lenses. The others called him Ray. The man sitting in the back with the boy was a very stocky and strong-looking man named Ben.

A wrinkled paper grocery sack in the middle of the rear seat contained what was left of sandwiches they had prepared for the journey. A large thermos contained enough coffee for each to have one more cup before they reached their destination, although the coffee would be cold by now.

The country they were driving through was flat and featureless, farm country, but the fields were devoid of life in the November chill. Occasionally a house could be seen back away from the highway, or a windmill, and sometimes a tree or two, stark against the empty landscape. Creosote-soaked telephone poles carrying power lines straight down the line of the highway were the only topographical feature most of the time.

Just before sunset, Tom pulled off the highway and drove a short distance onto a deserted dirt road that showed no sign of recent use. All of them got out, stretched, walked about, and relieved themselves. One opened the trunk of the 1954 Chevrolet sedan. Squeezed into the large trunk were ten army surplus gas canisters. Ray removed three of the canisters and poured the gasoline into the automobile's tank using a tin funnel that Ben held. When the tank was full, Ray returned the empty canisters to the trunk. The men

1

took sandwiches from the sack and ate hurriedly while standing, their backs turned into the chilling wind, mindful to put the waxed paper wrapping back into the sack to leave no evidence of their having been there. Fearful of someone chancing upon them, all four nervously scanned the dirt road as far as they could see. They had carried enough gas for the trip to eliminate the need to stop at a filling station and chance being seen and remembered, and had brought sandwiches for the same reason. The plan was to reach their destination, do their business, and drive back home without stopping except at deserted side roads like this one to refill their tank, giving no one the opportunity to remember them.

When the sandwiches and coffee were gone, Ray and the others got back into the car and started the final leg of their trip. It was well after dark when they found the road to the farm they sought and turned on to it. After bumping along a dirt road for almost a mile, a frame house flanked by a large barn came into view. Tom pulled the car into the driveway in front of the house, coasting the last few feet with the engine off for stealth. Light glowed in several of the windows in the house. The four men got out of the car and carefully eased the doors back until they made silent contact. Quietly raising the trunk lid again, Tom and Ray took out .30-30 Winchester carbines. As silently as possible, both levered rounds into the chambers and eased the hammer onto safety with their thumbs. There was a pause then, and the three men looked at each other as if to say, "Are we really ready to do this?" Ray nodded an affirmative to the unvoiced question, and Tom and Ben nodded in reply.

Ben whispered instructions to the boy to stay in the car, ready to drive during an escape if a speedy departure became necessary. Then the three men stepped quietly onto the porch. Tom reached up and unscrewed the bulb of the porch light. Taking a deep breath, Ben knocked loudly on the door.

Someone could be heard moving inside the house. A light came on in the area just inside the door, but thanks to the unscrewed bulb, the porch remained dark.

A white-haired man opened the door. An average-sized man with nondescript features, he wore denim bib overalls with a plaid shirt.

"Who's there?" the man demanded, trying unsuccessfully to see from the lighted interior to the darkened porch, squinting over the reading glasses worn low on his nose. "What do you want?"

With that Ray stepped around Ben and shoved the muzzle of the

Winchester into the man's chest in a distinctly ungentle manner.

"You'll find out soon enough what we want, you old bastard," Ray snarled, punctuating the remark with another jab of the gun barrel into the man's chest. "Where's your brother?"

"He's out in the kitchen," the man stammered. His eyes had widened and he stumbled backwards at the appearance of the gun. "Who are you? What do you want?"

"Move!" Ray commanded, prodding the man again.

The man backed unsteadily into the house and wobbled down a hall into the lighted room at the back of the house, followed closely by the three intruders, Ray with the gun pressed to the man's back.

Another man was seated at a small table in the kitchen, eating soup from a bowl. He was slightly smaller than the first man, and looked to be roughly the same age as the first. The second man also wore dirty overalls, and had long, disheveled white hair. His facial features were sharper, covered with what appeared to be several days' growth of white beard. A prominent Adam's apple began to bob up and down as he looked up when the first man was pushed roughly into the room. "What the hell—?" he exclaimed, but got nothing more out as Tom stepped forward and pushed the barrel of his Winchester to a point six inches in front of the man's nose.

"Jesus!" the second man said as he stared down the barrel of the rifle with wide eyes. "Who are you? What do you want?"

"Look at me real good you son of a bitch," Ray answered. "Do you remember me?"

Both of the frightened men seemed to look carefully at Ray for the first time, but recognition did not come. "What about me? Do you remember me, Jesse?" Tom said to the second man still sitting at the table. Then he turned to address the first man, standing unsteadily at the end of Ray's gun. "What about you, Lige? Think of me as a thirteen-year-old kid. Think of my sixteen-year-old sister. That might help you remember."

The two men were shocked to hear the intruding strangers use their names. They both looked more closely at the two gunmen, and recognition slowly began to register on the face of Jesse, sitting at the table, and then on Lige, and real fear began to show its ugly expression.

"Now wait," Jesse pleaded in a shaky voice. "That was twenty or thirty years ago. You can't come back at us now for that."

"It was yesterday for me you bastard," Ray snapped back. "Let's take a walk out to the barn to see what's changed out there. Get up!"

"No. Wait," Jesse started to plead.

"Goddamn it!" Ray exploded. "Get your sorry ass up and start moving or I'll blow your damn head off right here in your own kitchen."

Ben led the way, opening the back door and walking outside. Lige stumbled out behind him with Ray following closely, keeping the rifle barrel in contact with his back. Jesse got clumsily up, knocking the soup bowl off the table, and followed his brother on unsteady legs.

"Can't we just talk about this for a minute," Jesse pleaded. He appeared close to collapse from fear, but his begging provoked no sympathy from the intruders.

"We're going to talk about it all right," Ray spat. "Just like we talked about it when you two herded our sister and us out here. I used to beg too. Do you remember that? I begged you to leave her alone and let us go!"

Lige was near to tears. He kept whimpering, "Oh God. Oh God. Oh God," as he stumbled toward the barn.

"But I barely even remember that," Jesse whined.

"That's okay," Ray said. "I remember it good enough for both of us."

Ben, still in the lead, had reached the large door on the barn. The door was open, and a single light was on somewhere inside the large building, creating enough light for Ben to step inside and locate a bank of light switches. He began to flip the switches, and the inside of the barn was bathed in bright light from several bulbs on the ceiling and along the sides. The front half of the barn was open all the way to the roof trusses. Stalls on both sides from the middle to the back of the barn divided the side spaces into square cubicles. A loft ran around the entire barn roughly fifteen feet above the earthen floor. Bales of hay were stacked on the loft all the way around the barn. More hay was stored in most of the stalls. Ben pulled the sliding doors of the barn shut, first one side and then the other. When the second sliding door slammed into the first with a loud bang, Jesse cried out and fell to his knees.

"Get up!" Ray yelled. He grabbed the old man's shirt and roughly pulled him upright. "Now let's go back to the stall where you two used to rape my sister and whip Tom and me."

"I don't remember where," Lige whimpered. "It was so long ago."

"Then I guess I'll just shoot you here," Ray said. He pulled back the hammer on the Winchester. The click of the weapon cocking into firing mode sounded like thunder inside the barn.

"No wait," Lige hastily added. "I remember now." He walked unsteadily to the last stall on the right side. Jesse followed.

Using their rifles to prod and direct the two captives, Ray and Tom maneuvered them to the fence, standing in the next to last stall, facing into the last.

Ben took rope from a hook on the wall and pulled his pocket knife from his pocket. He cut pieces of the rope several feet long.

"Put your hands through the fence," Ray demanded, "just like you used to make us do."

When the two captives placed their hands through the fence Ben roughly tied their hands securely, and then looped the rope around the fence so that the two could not back away. He unbuttoned the shoulder flaps on their overalls and pulled the garments down below the trembling knees of the two farmers. Then he took lengths of the rope and tied a loop around their knees, connecting it to the fence. The two were now securely tied to the stall fence, their overalls down around their ankles revealing thin, bony white legs below boxer shorts on both men. Ben then went to the door and left the building. Those inside could hear a car start up and move to what sounded like just outside the door.

"This is the way you used to tie us while you did your business with our sister in that stall," Tom said, his voice shaking in anger. "How does it feel?"

"Tonight the bill comes due for that," Ray said. "You two are going to pay for what you did to our sister, and to us."

"Wait," Jesse begged. "We're sorry about what happened. We were young ourselves then. But we got some money now. You can have it if you let us go. We can all just forget this."

"When hell freezes over," Ray answered coldly.

Ben came back into the barn. He was carrying a coiled leather whip. He flipped it outward, and the leather snaked out almost ten feet.

"Let me go first," Ray said. "I've been waiting twenty-five years for this." He took the whip from Ben and positioned himself behind the two tied men. He pulled back his arm and arrayed the whip behind him, then lashed it forward. The whip tore through the still air in the barn with an evil hiss. Jesse screamed as the frayed leather tip tore through his underwear and buttocks. Lige began to cry and struggle wildly against his bindings, but he could not move away. The whip hissed through the air again and again, leaving angry red streaks on the two tied men from their upper legs to their upper back as they cried out in pain.

Their screams reverberated and seemed magnified inside the closed walls of the great barn.

"Please God! Please God!" Lige cried loudly.

"Stop! Please stop! I'm sorry, I'm sorry!" Jesse begged.

But Ray seemed lost in a furious rage and continued flailing away at the crying old men. Finally even Tom and Ben were repelled by his out-of-control rage, and both moved to stop him. Ben wrapped his arms around Ray from behind and held tight against his struggling, while Tom grabbed and held his wrist from the front. For a while Ray thrashed and made unintelligible sounds as tears of hurt and anger rolled down his cheeks.

"Ray! Ray!" Tom called to him. "Calm down. It's okay. Let one of us take our turn."

Slowly Ray calmed down and realized he had been out of control. He seemed to wilt in Ben's arms.

"I'm sorry. I'm sorry," Ray almost sobbed as he let Tom take the whip from his hands. "I guess I've kept that bottled up inside me for so long, it just came out all at once. I'm sorry."

"It's all right," Tom said soothingly. "I'm mad as hell too. Let me take my turn."

Tom took the whip and Ben led Ray to a spot out of the way. Ray sat on a bale of hay and stared at his hands as if wondering if they were his.

Tom lashed the two crying men several times and then Ben did the same, but Ray's loss of control and their having to stop him seemed to have taken much of the enthusiasm out of the act. Their lashes were hurtful, but nowhere near as vigorous as Ray's.

The backs of the two tied men were marked with angry red welts and cuts bleeding through their ripped shirts and shorts from their buttocks to their shoulders. They were both crying.

"Are you going to let us go now?" Lige whimpered.

"Hell no!" Tom said, "That part was for the times you tied Ray and me to the fence and beat us. Now you are going to pay for raping my sister over and over."

"What are you going to do to us?" Jesse sobbed.

"We're going to hang your sorry asses right here in your own barn," Ray answered coldly.

Chapter 2

The morning sun had not quite cleared the mountains when the man stepped onto the covered front porch of the small frame house. Blowing into a mug of coffee, he walked to the end of the porch and leaned against a support column. He sipped the hot coffee and stared out at a wide valley. To the left side of the valley as he looked out at it, a small town against impressive mountains was waking, electric lights glowing in ordered symmetry in the half-light of sunrise. To his right another distant range of mountains was just becoming visible at the edge of the retreating darkness. The wide valley, perhaps ten miles across, lay between the two mountain clusters. Behind and above the house rose two closer, almost identical mountains.

As the sun climbed over the mountains daylight spilled across the valley. The man smiled as he stood on his porch watching another day being born.

The man looked like what he was—a working cowboy. He wore jeans and well-worn riding boots with high heels and pointed toes, and a faded gray work shirt beneath a denim jacket. The man was slim, and the hands cupping the coffee mug were worn and scarred. His face was darkly tanned, but midway up his forehead the tan gave way to pale skin, the mark of a man who wore a hat when he worked.

Noticing a flicker of movement out of the corner of his eye, he looked to the right—toward the towering twin mountains—and saw a group of mule deer grazing on the upward slope, no more than fifty yards from his porch. There were ten in the group, one buck with an impressive rack of antlers, six does with no antlers, and three fawns, not much past the nursing stage. The man stood motionless, watching the grayish-brown deer graze, moving between small patches of grass growing on the rocky hillside. Periodically the deer would raise their heads to look for threats, and detecting none, lower them to continue grazing. The man felt lucky to be able to watch the reclusive deer from such close range. Not wanting to spook the skittish animals, he stood very still as he watched.

Eventually the horse in the nearby corral noticed the deer and snorted a startled exclamation that alarmed them. The deer rapidly bounded out of sight over a small rise on the slope. The man watched appreciatively as the deer nimbly ran and jumped over the rocky hillside. He smiled, tossed out the remaining coffee from his mug in an arching spray that sparkled in the morning sunlight as it fell through the air, and walked back into the house.

The house went dark as the lights that had created a warm orange glow in the windows were turned off. The man reemerged carrying a weathered, gray Stetson hat that he pulled down over his head. He walked stiffly on the high-heeled boots down the porch steps and across an open area that might be considered a yard. As he headed toward the corral, he passed a rock tank and a windmill.

The horse backed away at first when the man opened the gate. The man picked up a bridle hanging on the fence and approached the horse, which stilled as the familiar human talked soothingly to him. The man sped without thinking through the familiar ritual of saddling the horse, a process he had repeated countless times. He led the horse out of the corral, stopping to close the gate from habit, even though there were no other animals in the pen. He grasped the reins in one hand and the horn of the saddle in the other and pulled himself onto the horse's back. The horse took a couple of uneasy steps backward when he felt the weight, but quickly calmed.

There was a chill in the air. It was early October, and mornings in the mountain country were growing noticeably cooler. The man buttoned his denim jacket as he sat astride the horse. He paused to look once more out at the wide valley, and then back toward the tall twin mountains to his rear. Although the day was now bright, the shadows of house, windmill, and barn were still long. The dried white blossoms on the tall stalks rising out of the lechuguilla cactus plants growing on the upslope of the mountains glowed like torches in the direct sunlight. He looked up and saw a hawk riding the air currents high above, hunting.

"Lordy, it doesn't get any better than this, does it fella?" He often used the horse as an intermediary when talking to himself. Even though he had started almost every day of his adult life more or less in this same manner, he was still taken by the sharp beauty of a new dawn in this majestic mountain country. He never tired of it. Even if he had known that today was to be the last day of his life on this earth, he likely would have chosen to follow exactly the same routine.

"Well, horse," the man said, breaking his reverie, "I guess we'd better get started if we want to finish before sundown." Gently kicking the horse's flanks, he started the animal moving and steered him toward the twin mountains.

His work this day involved moving cattle—which had over the summer grazed higher and higher up on the mountains—back into the wide valley. For the next several hours he rode the horse in a wide arc across the faces of the two mountains, working down into every draw or ravine, and pushing Hereford cattle out of their hiding places in the brush downward off the mountains. By midday he had collected thirty animals and started them down the mountain.

The man stopped at a small spring to water and rest the horse, and to eat the lunch he'd packed before leaving the house. As he sat on a rock, listening to the water bubbling out from between two large rocks, he took a well-worn book of cowboy poetry from his saddlebag and read for a few minutes. He was tired, and would have liked to have stretched out on a large warm rock, pulled his hat over his eyes, and napped. But he wanted to get the cattle far out into the valley by the end of the day, so with a resigned groan, he prepared to resume herding the cattle toward the valley floor.

As he remounted, he felt a pain in his jaw and neck. Not much pain, more of a hint really, so he ignored it and continued riding. Soon, however, the sensation moved downward into his left arm, and became a dull ache. For a moment panic seized him, but he took deep breaths and consciously relaxed his neck and shoulders. Trying to move his upper body as little as possible, he gently turned the horse toward home, now over two miles away.

By the time he had traveled halfway to the house his chest felt as if an invisible belt was tightening around it. Gritting his teeth against the pain, the man rode on. When he was within one hundred yards of the house, he felt an intense, knifing pain in his chest. He gasped for air, clutched his chest, and fell off the horse. Landing heavily, he rolled onto his back, his hat falling from his head. He lay motionless for several moments. Then, half rising toward something only he saw, he gasped, "Daddy?"

Then the man closed his eyes, exhaled a long, slow last breath, and died. The horse stood nearby for a while, confused, but eventually walked the last few yards to the corral where he waited patiently for his human to come and feed him.

Chapter 3

Thinking about my childhood in rural West Texas was not something I had ever really done much of. To begin with, I did not have the type of personality that would lead me to contemplate my navel and ponder introspectively about how my experiences growing up had shaped my grown-up outlook on life. Nor did I have much awareness of, or interest in, my family history. Having consciously decided to leave what had been a distinctly rural upbringing and an early career in school teaching and coaching to pursue a more lucrative calling in hospital administration, I traded the country for the city, country people for city people, and kinfolk for business associates. I traded the underpaid teaching profession for the overpaid medical business—traded the past for the now, and had pretty much stopped thinking about the earlier times.

I still stayed in contact with a few friends from the old days, exchanged Christmas cards with them and a scattering of relatives every year, but our communications were short and mostly impersonal, not really actively engaged—just sort of doing what was socially required, but nothing more.

Looking back, I can pinpoint almost to the minute when that changed, when my family and its closets that turned out to be full of skeletons began to dominate my life. It was when I answered that telephone call from my secretary, just after two o'clock in the afternoon on the first Tuesday of October.

"Son Cable died?" I said. "That can't be right."

Sitting at my requisite over-sized desk in my office in the executive suites of the West Austin Medical Center, I had been staring mindlessly out across the live oak-covered, rolling hills to the west of Austin. An ugly, contentious meeting with the president of the medical staff and the chief of Obstetrics and Gynecology had just concluded. Anger and resentment still hung in the room like dust particles in a shaft of sunlight.

Another crisis was the last thing I needed at that moment, being smack in the middle of a major crisis in my career and a minor mid-life crisis in my personal life. At this stage of my "now" life, I had achieved what I had thought of, up to this point, as pretty solid success, having ascended to the position of chief executive officer of the West Austin Medical Center. However, it had come as something of a shock and disappointment to me that life in the top position was not as much fun or nearly as personally

11

satisfying as I had anticipated while on the way up, and—to top it off—this day had turned out to be a particularly unpleasant one.

The meeting with the two medical staff leaders had turned decidedly ugly when I told them that I would not support their dream of the women's health center they wanted to build adjacent to the hospital. For several months the two entrepreneurial medical chiefs had been lobbying to convince me to move women's services outside the main hospital into a separate, freestanding facility to be owned by physicians, with these two among the largest shareholders. Such a facility would undoubtedly make the physician owners rich, but it would be financially ruinous for the hospital. This clearly did not concern the physicians, who were focused only on their own potential enrichment.

"Doctors," I finally interrupted their arguments. "I understand why you want to do this. If I were in your place I would probably want to do it too, but as the CEO of this hospital I have to protect the interests of the hospital. The center you want to build would be very rewarding for you, but would be devastating to the hospital. I'm sorry, but I can't support the project, and I will have to strongly oppose it."

At that the two physicians became very angry and very energetic in proclaiming my lack of wisdom and vision. I knew this would not be the end of the debate. The employees of the hospital would regard such a decision by me as a final answer and accept it, but the physicians would not hesitate to take the argument over my head to my superiors, the board of directors, to seek a different answer. In some ways they were probably pleased at being able to take that route, because even had I supported the project I would have had to get board approval for the capital expenditures. They saw this as going directly to the real decision makers. Dealing with physicians in a hospital setting can be very frustrating. In lobbying for the project with board members, the physicians would undoubtedly call for a review of my continued employment as the CEO. This was almost a required maneuver in trying to intimidate the non-physician hospital CEO.

"I do not see how we, as physicians practicing here, can in good conscience continue to allow this institution to be led by an individual with so little vision. I can assure you the medical staff will find your stance intolerable." Dr. Howard, the president of the medical staff, had said as he angrily huffed out of my office. A small man with a large ego, Dr. Howard was in his first year as president, and anxious to wield the power of his position. In his early fifties, his gray hair was combed straight back, and his thin lips were nearly always compressed into a frown. It was if he felt the need to demonstrate his seriousness toward life in general and to emphasize the burden he carried on behalf of his medical colleagues.

"Unacceptable! Simply unacceptable!" Dr. Fine, the chief of Obstetrics and Gynecology, had whined as he minced out behind Dr. Howard. A man of medium size and build, Dr. Fine wore his graying hair cut in a flattop. He also wore big, black-framed eyeglasses, and a bow tie.

My decision to oppose their Women's Center had been a difficult one, and the meeting with the two physicians something I had dreaded. Few humans can be more pompous and full of themselves than physicians, and these two led the pack in vanity and ego.

I was fighting to control my temper and maintain an aura of professionalism. It was difficult. What I really wanted to say was, "Don't you two quacks have some patients you could perform some unnecessary tests on?"

But I just said, "It's unfortunate that you feel that way, but I cannot change my position on this. I have to look at what is best for the hospital."

Ultimately, to put an end to the tirade, I was forced to use my weapon of last resort, physical intimidation. A former college football player, I am six foot five and weigh over two hundred fifty pounds. Most physicians were the nerds or geeks of their school classes before their medical training, and lofty status in society allowed them to assume a superior, condescending attitude toward all non-physician muggles. However, by invading the personal space of most of the more obnoxious ones, I appear to summon forth uncomfortable memories of geeks having their pants run up the flagpole by high school jocks and bullies. Flashbacks to a time when they were on the low end of the social pecking order usually dissolve their condescending facade. When I stood and moved to their side of the desk, the two preening physicians quickly brought the meeting to a close and left. Since their departure I had been sitting at my desk and staring blankly out the window.

It was unlikely that the two angry physicians would find much support among the board members to overturn my decision—their project was predicted to siphon three to five million dollars per year out of the hospital revenue—but hospital boards fear conflict between administration and the medical staff. The turmoil the two vindictive physicians and their allies churned up would create unease among the board members. Eventually, when enough unease was created, the board would acquiesce to their demand for my removal. Such is the inevitable fate of a hospital CEO, whose job security is somewhat less than that of a major-league baseball manager. Hospital boards theoretically control and govern the physicians who work at a hospital, but those same physicians control the revenue of the hospital by admitting patients. If physicians withhold admissions, the hospital suffers financially. Hospital boards hire professional administrators to manage the hospital, and the physicians, but when conflict builds between the administrator and the physicians, the board usually mollifies the physicians by changing administrators.

I sat at my desk staring out the large window, waiting for my blood pressure to drop back down to within shouting distance of high, and for the queasy feeling in my stomach to subside. I rose and walked into a small bathroom off the office, washed my face in the sink and stared into the mirror. I did not like what I saw. The eyes looked tired. Around the temples, there was more gray showing in the brown hair than I remembered. There was a slump in the shoulders, and there seemed to be more weight around the waist than the last time I had looked. The man looking out at me had definitely lost the athletic body of youth. This was a guy who was beginning to look old, and tired. Who the hell was this old guy?

Reentering the office and sitting down heavily at the desk, I felt exhausted. I closed my eyes and practiced slow, deep breathing. As I began to put the meeting out of my mind, the telephone on my desk rang, startling me. Recovering, I punched the appropriate button and said, "Yes?"

"I'm sorry to bother you, Mr. Carter," Mrs. Robinson, my secretary, said. "But during your meeting your Aunt Frances called. May I come in for a minute to tell you about her call?"

"Sure. Come on in," I replied, but I did not like the sound of this. My Aunt Frances had never called me at work, and in recent years the only time I heard from her had been to relay bad news about various aging relatives. In spite of my reluctance to get involved, Aunt Frances seemed to think it was her God-sworn family duty to keep me informed.

Jane Robinson came into my office and closed the door behind her. In her early fifties, Jane was a pleasant-looking woman of average size, her short cropped hair beginning to trend toward gray.

Jane said, "I'm very sorry to tell you this, but your Aunt Frances wanted you to know that a relative, John Wesley Cable, passed away. She said he was someone you were very close to as a child. The funeral will be in Alpine this Saturday. Would you like for me to start making arrangements for you to go?"

I thought for a minute and then said, "Son Cable died? That can't be right."

"Son? She called him John Wesley. Was he her son?" Jane asked.

"No," I replied. "John Wesley Cable is, was, his given name. Son was his nickname."

"Son? Do you mean Son as in son of the father, or Sun as in sunshine?"

"Son of the father," I said.

"That's an unusual nickname. How did he get it?"

"The story is that when his father, Ben Cable, took him to the barbershop the first time one of the regulars asked, 'Who's this?' John Wesley puffed up his chest and proudly announced, 'I'm Son and he's Daddy.' The barbershop regulars got a big kick out of that, and all of them started calling him Son. The nickname just stuck with him after that. It got around town and everyone started calling him Son. A lot of people also called Ben 'Dad' Cable after that." I grinned as I remembered the story.

"What a beautiful story," Jane said.

"Did she say how he died?"

"His family believes it was a heart attack. She seemed to think you would want to go to the funeral."

"No," I said. "He was just a cousin. I actually haven't seen him in years." I answered without really thinking. In the executive world a death in your immediate family would be only marginally acceptable as an excuse to miss work—cousins were not even on the radar.

"Your aunt was sure you would want to go. She said they were having something special, a cowboy's funeral is what she called it."

"My Aunt Frances was a lot closer to that branch of the family than I was. And besides, we have to prepare for the board meeting next Monday, and the finance committee meets this Friday. There's no way I could take off now. I'll just send flowers or something." I sagged back in my chair, very tired.

"Are you sure?" Jane said. "We can get by without you for a few days. Don't you think they need you, and you need them at a time like this?"

"You don't understand," I said, somewhat defensively. "My family is different. They're very country, and way past eccentric. I left that part of the world a long time ago. I wouldn't fit in even if I did go back."

"Family is family," Jane said, as if delivering the final verdict. "I'm sure they would be glad to see you, and you them."

"No." I rejected her verdict. "That's a different world out there."

"All right. I'll take care of the flowers for you," she said. Her voice dripped disapproval as caustic as battery acid. I winced in spite of myself.

I had half an hour before a scheduled meeting with the chief of the radiology department. Dr. Howard Kerley wanted to purchase a new high-tech, mega-million dollar diagnostic imaging machine. The new machine would enable physicians to see inside the human body with more clarity and efficiency than all of the other mega-million dollar machines the medical center already owned, and, more importantly, would allow the radiologists to charge even more extravagant fees for looking at and interpreting the pictures that the machine would produce.

Picking up his proposal, I tried to skim through it, but found it harder and harder to concentrate. Images, sounds, and even smells of hot, still summer days and cool nights spent listening to rain drumming on a tin roof had begun sneaking into the edges of my thoughts like fog seeping under the edges of a tent.

"Lizard graveyards!" I suddenly exclaimed, startling myself, and then I laughed out loud. "Lash LaRue," I said with a wide foolish grin. I thought for a few more moments, and then reached for the telephone.

"Mrs. Robinson," I said. "Call Dr. Kerley, and tell him something has come up. I won't be able to keep our meeting time. See if you can reschedule it sometime next week."

"Yes sir," she replied.

Leaning back, hands clasped behind my head, I stared out the large window, past the parking lot, toward a place and time far beyond the nearby hills. I began to actively remember an almost forgotten summer filled with experiences that now seemed like dreams, and of cousins, lots of cousins. I remembered Son Cable.

Chapter 4

"Who wants to go first?" Son asked. At twelve, he was the oldest of the seven male cousins gathered on the hillside. Being the oldest gave him the authority to make the final decision. He was a slender kid, long limbed, brown hair cropped close, a straw cowboy hat on his head.

"I do," Charlie quickly spoke up. Charlie was Son's youngest brother, ten that summer, the best athlete of the group and the usual champion of almost every game. Blond hair and blue eyes topped a build that was lean and lithe.

"Me too," Roy Don said. Eleven-year-old Roy Don was the middle brother, shorter than Charlie, red headed, freckled, and pugnacious.

The cousins had pulled the soap box derby racers we had spent most of the week building to the top of the railway bed along the backside of the Cable property. Where the railroad skirted the side of the mountains, and was cut partially into the grade, a long slope of dirt and gravel extended downward for over one hundred feet. This was our race track. We had discovered that a homemade racer would roll at breakneck speeds down the dirt slope and go some distance out onto the plains below. We called the area Mount Cable.

My cousins and I had soapbox derby races every chance we got that summer. We built the racers from scrap lumber found or scrounged from construction projects around town. A two-by-twelve-inch plank about four feet long made a perfect base for a racer, and two boards about three feet long were attached at cross-angles to the front and the back ends for wheel braces. The front wheel brace was secured with a single bolt in the center so that the front wheels could be pushed left and right by the feet of the rider, providing some degree of steerage. Metal pipes served as axles for the wheels. We tried many types of wheels, any type we could find. Bicycle wheels worked best, so we were constantly scrounging junkyards for old bicycle wheels.

A racer would support the weight of one rider sitting on the main body board with his feet on the front axle board. We tied a piece of rope to the front of the vehicle to give the rider something to hang on to. When we had two or more vehicles in working condition, we'd hold a race. On this special day we had three working racers. We pulled the racers to the top of the slope, with the back wheels against the railroad track. A rider would mount each vehicle. At a signal from a starter, an assistant would push the vehicle and rider off the edge, and the racers would roll and bounce crazily down the side of the railroad fill, and—if they reached the bottom—coast for some distance across the level prairie. There were two categories of winners; one was the fastest down, and the second was the one who traveled the greatest distance.

"I want to ride one," I said excitedly. I was eight that summer, already tall for my age, and heavier built than the other cousins.

"Me too! Me too!" Dewayne said. Dewayne, also eight, was the oldest son of my father's sister, Frances.

"Let's make the first race for the Cable family championship," Son said, ending the discussion with a diplomatic decision. "Then on the second race Tommy and Dewayne can take on the winner." There were two other cousins present. Robert Earl, my uncle Ray's son, was my age. A pale, effeminate boy, he never volunteered to ride, and we still considered Billy Rex, Dewayne's younger brother, too young at six. Billy Rex complained about not getting to ride, but Robert Earl seemed content to watch and help.

Son, Charlie, and Roy Don each quickly grabbed a racer. They climbed onto the vehicles, put their feet on the front axle board, and grabbed the steer rope with both hands. I got behind Roy Don to help him start, and Dewayne got behind Son. Robert Earl and Billy Rex made ready to push Charlie off the edge.

"When I count to three, push us over," Son said to the pit crews. I put both hands on Roy Don's back and braced one foot against a railroad tie to give myself something to push against.

"One. Two. Three!" Son said. I pushed as hard as I could against Roy Don's back, and he and the soap box racer went over the edge. "Yeehaaa!" he screamed as he plummeted down the slope, quickly gathering speed.

The others had pushed Son and Charlie over the edge. "Wahoooo!" Charlie yelled in exultation. Son did not scream. He tried to concentrate on steering his racer down the hill.

The three of them made the first third of the way down the hill more or less evenly, spewing dust and gravel. Suddenly Roy Don's front wheels struck some larger rocks, and his entire racer became airborne. While he was in the air, the front of the racer tipped downward and the front end struck heavily on the fill and buried into the slope. The rear of the racer flipped over the front, and Roy Don was thrown forward face first onto the slope. He hit hard and slid down the hill on his stomach, his face digging into the dirt, for several feet. The racer tumbled off to one side and settled on its back.

Son made it almost all the way to the bottom before his racer swerved wildly to the left and began to tumble in a sideward roll, carrying Son with it for several rolls before he separated from the vehicle. He rolled to a stop while the racer actually landed upright and pointing forward. It rolled riderless down the rest of the slope and a few feet out on the flat ground.

Charlie managed to ride his racer all the way down the hill and screamed and pumped his fists triumphantly as he coasted almost fifty feet out onto the flat ground.

"Dadgummit! Shoot!" Roy Don shouted angrily as he spit dirt out of his mouth. His nose trickled blood, and his lip appeared to be cut. He spit blood and blew dirt-filled mucus from his nose. "Dang it! Dang it! Dang it!" He pounded the ground with his fist.

Roy Don hated losing—particularly to Charlie, with whom he competed fiercely.

Son was laughing wildly as he lay on the ground. "That was so great!" he said between giggles.

"The champion! I'm the champion!" Charlie gleefully yelled as he jumped from his racer and ran back to check on Roy Don. Son also got up and moved to Roy Don, who had assumed a sitting position on the side of the hill, still spitting and complaining loudly. "Dadgummit! I had you beat till I hit those rocks."

"Let me see your nose," Son said. He inspected Roy Don's nose and seemed satisfied. "I think you're okay. Looks like you just got a little split lip and a nose bleed as usual." Roy Don was our bleeder. His nose would bleed at the drop of a hat, and he always seemed to find a way to lose enough skin to create a wound. He was tough though, and the sight of his own blood never seemed to concern him as much as it did the rest of us. Son once said Roy Don could find a way to bleed from eating an ice cream cone.

"I'm okay," Roy Don said as he got up. "Let's get the next race started. I want to take Charlie on again. I'll give either of you a dime if you let me take your ride in the next race," he said to Dewayne and me, who had joined them on the slope.

"No way," I quickly replied.

"Not me," Dewayne chimed in.

"Dang it! Dadgummit!" Roy Don said. He helped me pull the racer he had ridden back to the top of the hill. Despite his spectacular wreck, the vehicle seemed to be in workable condition. Our cousins pulled the other two racers back up the hill.

"Let's move over a little," Roy Don said when we had reached the top. "There's a buried rock or something I hit. Try to stay away from my tracks as you go down."

We placed the three racers against the tracks once more while Charlie, Dewayne, and I settled into place on them. Son got set to push Dewayne while Billy Rex got behind Charlie. Roy Don crouched behind me. "Don't let the wheels get turned," he said as last minute advice.

Son counted down again and Roy Don pushed hard against my back, launching me over the edge. I quickly gathered speed. It seemed the world was racing past me in a blur as I gained momentum. I was aware of a commotion to my right, but could not look in that direction. I hit a rock with the right front wheel. The racer tilted crazily to the left, and I was sure I was going to crash, but then the right wheel went back down and made contact with the ground. Somehow I avoided losing control, and the racer continued down the slope. The ground beneath me was a blur. I heard a loud yell to my left. Suddenly I hit the level ground at the bottom of the hill. The racer leveled out and I coasted forward, still moving at a good rate of speed. As I was no longer in danger of turning over, I quickly looked to the right and then to the left. I was by myself—the only one who had made it to the bottom of the hill. I had won! It was the first time I had ever won a race. When the racer slowed to a stop, I turned to see what had happened.

Dewayne had crashed about half way down the slope. A wheel had fallen off his vehicle, and Dewayne was sitting on the slope gingerly rubbing his elbow. He was covered with dirt, appearing to have rolled several times. Charlie had made it almost all the way down before disaster stuck. Both front wheels had come off his racer, and the wheels had been mauled in the crash following their exit. Charlie was rubbing the top of his head. He looked about with a quizzical expression that seemed to say, "That's not supposed to happen."

"Way to go Tommy!" Roy Don whooped as he raced down the hill to congratulate me. "You beat Charlie! Way to go!"

I was shocked—not just that I had won—but that I had beaten Charlie. He never lost at anything. It was an exhilarating feeling.

Son inspected Dewayne and Charlie and pronounced them well enough to continue. Dewayne was bruised a little from his tumbling, and Charlie had a bump on his scalp, but neither was seriously hurt. We turned our attention back to the racers.

The racer Charlie had wrecked was beyond repair. The cross-brace for the front wheels had broken cleanly in two, and the front wheels were mangled. The vehicle Dewayne had wrecked was missing one wheel, but the rest of the craft was serviceable enough. We quickly salvaged one of the rear wheels from Charlie's wreck and repaired Dewayne's vehicle. We had two racers, but who should take the next ride?

"I'm defending champion," I said, staking my claim to a racer.

"But I won the race before that," Charlie said.

"I haven't gotten to the bottom ever," Dewayne said. "It's still my turn since I haven't finished yet."

"Me and Charlie. Grudge match," Roy Don said in a voice that halted all the conversation. Charlie and Roy Don were extremely competitive. Charlie was the more gifted athlete, and seemed to win more often, but Roy Don was the more determined of the two, and won his share of contests on will alone.

"I'd kinda like to see that," Dewayne said.

"Yeah, me too," I said. Watching the two of them go head to head was almost as much fun as doing something myself. Besides, I had won a race today, my first, and I wanted to finish the day on that note. I did not want to chance losing the next race. I wanted to go home a winner.

"Oh all right," Son said. "Let's get the cars back up the hill."

We pulled the racers back to the top. Charlie and Roy Don assumed racing position. We decided to double up on pushing them at the start. Son and Billy Rex got behind Charlie while Robert Earl and I took a position behind Roy Don. "Push me as hard as you can," Roy Don whispered to us as Son began the count.

When Son said, "Three," Robert Earl and I strained as hard as we could and launched Roy Don off the edge. Son and Billy Rex seemed to give just as much effort in starting Charlie. Both racers went over the edge with such force that they actually took flight, sailing through the air for a few seconds before crashing back to the surface. It was too much momentum. When the racers hit the ground the impact caused both riders to lose control. The vehicles veered sharply into one another. The front wheels became interlocked and the racers immediately began tumbling. All four wheels flew off Charlie's racer while the front two sailed off Roy Don's racer, rolling down the hill. The frames dug into the ground and the back ends were catapulted over the front, throwing Charlie and Roy Don some distance down the hill. The two boys landed rolling and tumbling down the hill. It was a spectacular crash.

"Wow!" I exclaimed.

"Cool!" Dewayne said in wonder.

When he stopped rolling Roy Don immediately leapt up in anger, fists clenched. "You ran into me on purpose," he claimed. "I'm gonna punch you out!"

Charlie, however, did not respond in kind. He was sitting on the hill clutching his right forearm as a small amount of blood oozed from an ugly welt. Roy Don, upon seeing his brother's wound, immediately lost all anger. He whipped a handkerchief from his pocket and tightly wrapped it around the forearm. By the time the rest of us had gotten down the hill Roy Don had effectively bandaged the wound, and he and Charlie were laughing together as they recounted the spectacular crash. It was indeed the best crash any of us could remember.

Both remaining vehicles had been destroyed in the crash. The races were concluded due to no vehicle being in working order. We gathered up all the pieces we could carry and walked back to the Cable house. I appeared to be the only one with no significant wound, and I had won my only race. What a day! Even some forty-odd years later, I still remembered it as one of the best days of my life.

Chapter 5

"Mrs. Robinson," I said as I bounced into the outer office, "I've changed my mind. I am going to my cousin's funeral. I'll be back in time for the board meeting on Monday."

"Yes sir," Mrs. Robinson smiled, making no attempt to conceal her pleasure at my having finally made what she considered to be the correct decision—no doubt because of her insistence.

Wednesday sped by as I prepared for the trip and my absence from the hospital. Robert Blake, vice president and chief financial officer, would chair the finance committee meeting in my absence. Eager for the opportunity to be seen as a man ready for the top job, Blake worked hard to assure me that I had made the right decision, and that he could handle the responsibility. In his early forties, Blake was at the peak of his upwardly mobile years. He was constantly seeking opportunities to curry favor with board or medical staff members. A small man with a large "little man syndrome," Blake had a pallid complexion and wore the trendy circular wire-frame spectacles that were currently in vogue with yuppie America. His dark brown hair was turning gray at the temples, and he actually got a manicure every time he went to his hair stylist. He worked hard to look the part of a corporate CEO, and I had no doubt he was already campaigning for the job. Blake had been a holdover from the previous CEO's staff. I had retained him to provide a degree of continuity. In retrospect, because he had no loyalty to me, keeping him had probably not been a good decision. But the desire to move up was common in a field dominated by aggressive individuals. I could not fault him for having ambition. Together we prepared the agenda for the finance committee meeting. His main job was to make sure the committee understood the folly of the women's hospital scheme pushed by Doctors Fine and Howard.

Controlling the agenda was a tremendous advantage in dealing with combative constituencies. When I prepared the agenda and supporting material for the board of directors meeting scheduled for Monday, I scheduled Doctors Fine and Howard immediately after the chief financial officer's report on the dismal financial prospects of their proposal. When Blake detailed the huge projected losses of the project, the two physicians' complaints about my lack of vision would have little credibility. Their pleadings would not find receptive ears.

My family had been very supportive of my taking a few days off to go to the funeral when I had announced the event at dinner the previous evening.

"How was work today?" my wife Kathy had asked.

Kathy was well aware of my growing disenchantment with my job, and she was concerned that stress and age were taking their toll on me. I told her about my meeting with Dr. Fine and Dr. Howard that had ended in anger and resentment.

"A trip out to West Texas will be good for you," Kathy said. "Get away from that job and hospital for awhile. Have you thought any more about leaving?"

We had talked from time to time about moving back to a smaller town and a simpler life. Kathy had actually attended a one-room school in the tiny town in New Mexico where she grew up. She had never been comfortable in the larger cities as I pursued my career. She often talked about the joys and freedom of growing up in the country, of owning a horse she could ride for miles in any direction. We had started our married life in more rural settings. After college graduation, I spent several years as a high school teacher and football coach. Kathy was a new graduate nurse when we met. A few years into our marriage I began to dream of a career that would provide more financial security for my family, so I went back to school for a graduate degree and moved into health care administration. The larger hospitals in the larger cities held more opportunity for me, so I evolved from a small-town coach into a big-city hospital executive. We had spent time living in Dallas and Fort Worth before the current job in Austin. In spite of the physical relocation, Kathy had never fully gotten away from her country roots. But I always took the position that the financial rewards were such that it would be unfair to the family—Kathy, eleven-year-old Alice, fourteen-year-old Renee, and sixteen-year-old Jonathan—to go to a less rewarding post. Kathy felt certain we would all quickly adjust.

"Yeah, I've thought about it," I said, and let the subject die.

We decided against taking the kids out of school, so Kathy would stay in Austin with them. She saw the trip as something of a vacation for me. She felt that getting away for a few days, even under these less than ideal circumstances, would be good for me.

Chapter 6

A man was filling portable gas cans from a large storage tank behind the barn. The tank sat on a welded frame six feet above the ground. Gravity was all that was required to drain gasoline from the storage tank into the cans which were sitting in the back of a pickup truck, but it was a slow process. The man waited patiently as each can was topped off, ten in all. Then he took several elastic bungee cords and secured the cans en masse to the front of the truck bed to prevent them moving around during the trip. The pickup was a double cab Ford, perhaps two or three years old, white, and covered with dirt and mud from the dirt roads on the farm.

Getting into the truck, the man started it up and pulled around the barn and drove to the front of the house. He got out and went into the house, only to reappear a few minutes later carrying two cloth duffel bags which he tossed onto the rear seat. As he was loading the bags, a second man came from the house. This man appeared to be slightly older than the first. He carried two rifles and a long western-style revolver in a holster. All the weapons were carefully placed under the rear seat.

"Did you get all the gas cans filled?" the older man asked.

"Yep. They're all full and secured. We're ready to go," was the answer. The younger of the two wore a full beard that was beginning to turn gray. Both men were dressed in ranch work clothes—jeans, work shirts, boots, and western hats.

"Well," the older man said, "we've got four hundred miles to cover. Let's get to bed early tonight and leave before daylight in the morning."

"Sounds like a plan to me," the younger man said, and the two of them walked back into the white frame farmhouse.

Chapter 7

At nine o'clock on Thursday morning I pulled out of our driveway in my red Dodge Ram pickup truck, and headed for West Texas. The truck had been my middle-aged crazy present to myself. I did not realize at the time that it connected me back to my rural youth in West Texas. It just seemed more manly than the minivans and sports cars driven by the other executives in my neighborhood. Even as a semi-successful big-city hospital executive, I still subscribed to the regional attitude that in Texas a real man ought to drive a truck. Shortly after turning fifty I saw the truck in the sales lot and fell in love. In Texas we like to say that when we have a mid-life crisis we don't get a sports car and a teenaged girlfriend like our counterparts in the North—we buy a new truck and go hunting. I had the truck, now all I needed was the hunting.

Heading west on Highway 290 to the sound of Willie Nelson singing "On the Road Again" on the radio, I was already starting to unwind and feel better as I sang along.

My improved attitude this morning was shared by many Texans simply because it was late October. We'd made it through summer, and the weather was starting to cool down. We Texans love our state, but even the most zealous have to admit that the place is damned near uninhabitable in July, August, and September, when temperatures reach well over one hundred degrees, day after day. Just going about life's daily activities sucks all the energy out of you. By mid-September most of us were stuck in a perpetual slow motion trance. Then—finally—October arrived, and spirits rose as the temperature dropped. I've always imagined hearing trumpet flourishes or Beethoven's "Ode to Joy" blowing in the winds of the season's first cold front, so elevating is the relief of having lived through another summer.

The drive from Austin to West Texas took me through some of the most interesting geologic areas of Texas. Austin was located just south of the geographic center of the state, astride a fault line called the Balcones Fault. This prehistoric faulting separated the flat Coastal Plain of Texas from the Hill Country of Texas, two distinct geological environments. Austin, sitting directly on the fault, was a city with flat plains in its eastern half and rocky hills in its western half. Those hills, composed of massive accumulations of limestone, wrinkled the landscape westward for four hundred miles into the Pecos River region of far West Texas. Elevations rose from around four hundred feet at Austin to over four thousand feet in the west. Over centuries, water from springs, creeks, and rivers near Austin has dissolved the limestone and created a ruggedly beautiful landscape, referred to as the Hill Country of central Texas. Most Texans regarded the Hill Country as one of the most attractive areas of the state; perhaps second only to the area that was my final destination on this trip.

The road wound through limestone hills covered with thick stands of live oak trees and native grasses, over picturesque creeks and rivers. The area was mostly ranching country. Native whitetail deer and wild turkey flourished in the limestone canyons and armadillos, the shy little armored animals that have become a popular, if unofficial, symbol of Texas in recent years, are also abundant.

After zipping through the tiny hamlet of Dripping Springs, I passed through Johnson City, the hometown of former President Lyndon Baines Johnson, and then Fredericksburg, a quaint old German town that was the latest small town to be "discovered" by developers and become overcrowded.

West of Fredericksburg the highway followed what was once the Butterfield stagecoach route from San Antonio to El Paso. As I cruised down the highway, singing, watching the white lines of the highway disappear beneath my truck, my mind wandered backward again.

Chapter 8

"Wake up sleepy-head! Are you going to sleep all day?" My mother's voice roused me from a deep and comforting sleep.

"Is Daddy still here?" I asked as I rolled over to look sleepily at her. I loved to sit at the kitchen table with my father while he drank coffee in the morning before leaving for work.

"No. He left almost an hour ago. Get up and I'll fix you some breakfast."

Since my father was already gone I was in no hurry to get up. Rolling back toward the wall, I looked out the open window next to my bed. The windmill was turning lazily, and I could hear water splashing into the metal tank on a rock base near the windmill. My window was on the east side of the house, and the sun was just topping a tall mountain. In a very short time the sun would warm this side of the house and the area next to the window where my bed was located, but for the moment the cool of the night hung on, and I snuggled beneath a quilt and listened to the windmill. I loved listening to the windmill. The rhythmic creaking and the chattering of water into the tank put me to sleep every evening. There was a sense of continuance and comfort in the sounds.

My father worked as a carpenter, a profession that required our family to move frequently. In rural West Texas there was seldom a steady supply of construction projects in any one area, so we moved from town to town as jobs became available. That summer—when I was eight and my sister was six—we were living in Alpine, Texas. We had rented a small stucco house about half a mile from the house of our cousins, the Cables. We'd lived in a succession of rent houses, and this was one of the better ones. A wide, covered porch across the front provided shade in the afternoon. The windmill and water tank in the back fascinated and entertained me endlessly. I remember the sound of the windmill as it turned in the wind, and the reassuring sound of water splashing into the tank. Even now I hear those sounds at night as I drift between sleep and awareness. In my dreams there always will be a windmill whispering to me from outside my bedroom window.

"There's some bacon left," my mother said from the kitchen. "Do you want eggs this morning?"

"Yes," I answered as I reluctantly rolled away from my windmill window and climbed out of bed. I walked sleepily to the kitchen and took a place at the small table, brushing thick reddish-brown hair from my face, revealing a spattering of freckles. I took a piece of bacon from a plate on the table and began to chew it vigorously. My mother was frying eggs in bacon fat at the stove.

"Do you want to go to the Cable's house today?" my mother asked as she placed a plate with two fried eggs in front of me. "I've got to mop, and it would be good if you two stay over there for awhile, till everything dries."

"Okay," I said, as I attacked the eggs, not bothering to hide my grin. "Can we stay the whole day?" Playing at the Cable's house was always fun.

"If Arva doesn't mind feeding you," she replied as my sister came into the room and turned her nose up at the eggs I was eating. My sister's name was Betty Jean, but everyone had evolved from calling her "Sister" to "Sissy."

"I want cereal," Sissy said petulantly, as she plopped down in the chair opposite me.

My mother fetched a box of cornflakes and a bottle of milk. "Just be home in time for supper," she said. That would be about seven in the evening, at least an hour before dark. My father would get home at six-thirty and would be hungry after a day of physical labor. We tried to eat as soon as possible after he came home.

Following breakfast, Sissy and I changed into summer clothes—jeans, sneakers, and a cotton shirt for me, a loose-fitting summer dress with old, brown penny loafers for her. Sissy pulled her blonde hair into a ponytail, and I also strapped on my holster and cap gun pistol, wearing it low in gunfighter style.

The walk to the Cable's house took us down a dirt road bordered on both sides by wire fences. We lived just outside the edge of the town, and development was sparse. We only passed two houses on our half-mile trip. One of them was the small wood frame house rented by Uncle Ray.

The summer had barely begun when my father's brother Ray secured work at the same construction project as my father and moved his family to Alpine. An affable man, Ray had married an unpleasant woman named Hilda, and they had three children.

Their oldest child was Robert Earl, a boy my age. A slender, almost frail kid, Robert Earl had adopted many girlish mannerisms. This was a time before homosexuality was openly discussed. Our parents never talked about it, and we were too young to understand anyway. We accepted Robert Earl as our cousin, even though we thought it strange that he many times preferred to play with the girls.

Ray's next child was Aloe, a girl of seven. Aloe was a skinny kid with dark hair always worn in pigtails. She was loud and aggressive, wanting to be the leader in every game. Blossom, at six, was a constant whiner, always hanging back and delaying every adventure.

There was no sign of activity as Sissy and I passed, so we kept going. As we walked I picked up rocks from the road and practiced throwing them at fence posts and bushes. I was excited to be heading for a day of play, and could barely restrain the urge to break into an exuberant run. Sissy continually complained about the walk, and stopped frequently to empty pebbles from her penny loafers.

When we finally arrived at the Cable house, we went to the screened porch at the back of the house and entered through the screen door. The door into the kitchen in the rear of the house was open, and Aunt Arva was sitting at the table picking beans.

"Hi Aunt Arva," I said. "My mom said we could stay over here all day if it was okay with you."

Aunt Arva looked tiredly at me and said, "I guess it's okay if you behave yourselves. The boys are out back somewhere around the cow pen, and the girls are in their bedroom."

Arva was my father's sister. Her given name was Arvazene, but everyone called her Arva. She had married an itinerant cowboy named Ben Cable who—following marriage and kids—found steadier work driving a delivery truck. Ben and Arva had five children. The oldest was Son (John Wesley), who was twelve that summer. He was a tall kid who had inherited his father's dream of being a cowboy. His sandy hair was always capped with a straw cowboy hat. The second oldest son, Roy Don, had such a high energy level that he darted about like a water bug. Even at ten, Charlie was built like an athlete, and he moved with a natural grace and agility that foretold his future as a professional athlete. He was also the best-looking, and knew he was special even then.

Eight-year-old Starlene was the oldest daughter. We shortened her name to Star. Star always seemed mature before her time, often more like the adults than the rest of the kids. The baby of the family was six-year-old Crystal, who followed her siblings about being unbearably cute, a cheerleader and prom queen in the making.

Ben "Dad" Cable had acquired a small piece of land on the western edge of Alpine, and built a house with his own hands. The house had three bedrooms. The three boys slept in one, the two girls in a second. Ben and Arva occupied the third bedroom. There was one bathroom, a kitchen, and a living room. A screened-in porch across the back of the house was used as a dining room in hot weather, and the kids often moved their beds onto the porch to sleep. It was a small home for seven people, but I never remember feeling crowded there, no matter how many relatives came to visit. That summer was a good example. Dewayne and Billy Rex were currently staying at the Cable house. Frances, my father's youngest sister, and her husband Henry, had needed some time away from the boys, so they arranged to have their two sons summer with the Cables in Alpine. It was common practice then among relatives for children to spend weeks or even months with another branch of the family. That respite from child care substituted for a vacation for parents too poor to be able to take time off from work or vacation trips.

Dewayne, the oldest, was my age. He was a short, chubby kid, with a pointed face and dark hair. He also had the brightest mind in the group, always the first to discover a flaw in a plan or find a way to escalate the mischief. His brother Billy Rex, two years younger, was a shy kid who followed Dewayne around like a puppy. Billy Rex had thin, blond hair and wore thick glasses even at that young age.

It's probably accurate to describe all of us as closer to poor than middle class, but we always had plenty to eat—even though beans were usually the main course—and clothes to wear, although they were often second-hand or hand-me-downs with multiple patches. All of the kids—including me—were blissfully ignorant of our actual status in the socioeconomic structure of Alpine, Texas. We just spent those summer days playing with our cousins and thinking life couldn't be much better.

Sissy went off to the girls' bedroom to join Star and Crystal. I went out back in search of the boys. I usually gravitated toward Charlie, and we had a well-established routine.

As I hurried toward the cow pen I was stopped dead in my tracks by a slow, chilling voice saying, "Hold it right there stranger. We don't like strangers around here. You look like an outlaw to me. I think maybe I'd better plug you right now."

Slowly turning toward the voice, I was relieved that I had remembered to come armed. Charlie was leaning against the fence next to the small barn. He was also armed, a cap pistol strapped low on his hip. His hand hovered above the handle in threatening readiness. He stepped away from the fence toward me.

"I think maybe I'll just plug you," I said, accepting the challenge. "I plan to stay in these parts."

"We'll have to see about that," Charlie said grimly as he moved ominously toward me.

We stalked each other like the gunfighters we had seen in countless Saturday matinees. I tried to make myself focus on his eyes because some Saturday gunfighter had said you could tell when a man was going to reach for his gun by watching his eyes. We stopped about twenty feet apart.

"Draw," Charlie said coldly.

"You draw," I said in a voice I hoped was colder.

We went for the pistols strapped to our hips, drew, and fired.

"Bang! Bang!" we both loudly shouted.

Suddenly I realized that he had miraculously gotten off a shot that knocked the gun right out of my hand at the very instant I had done exactly the same thing to him.

"Ouch!" I cringed, dropping my pistol and shaking my jolted gun hand in surprise.

"Ouch!" Charlie exclaimed, also dropping his pistol and shaking his hand in pain.

"Say, you're mighty fast, stranger," I said in wonder.

"So are you," Charlie said. "Say partner, maybe we'd better team up to fight outlaws since neither of us can outshoot the other."

"Sounds good to me, partner," I agreed, and the two unbeatable gunslingers started another exciting day of fighting rustlers, bank robbers, and other assorted villains. It was a routine we seldom varied from that summer.

Chapter 9

The two men had been driving mile after empty mile for almost four hours and they were still in the vast Texas Panhandle—flat, almost featureless country except for windmills and telephone poles. They had risen before dawn, eaten breakfast, and left home just as the sun was coming up. They had been traveling in thoughtful silence.

"Do you think we're doing the right thing?" the younger man in the passenger seat suddenly asked the older man, who was driving.

"Doesn't matter," the driver replied. "A promise is a promise, and family is family. We gave our word we'd do it, and we will."

"Do you believe it even exists?" the younger man continued. "And if it does, will we be able to find it? And if we do find it, what are our chances of getting away with it without some kind of confrontation?"

"Well, I reckon that's why we're carrying guns, isn't it," the driver said without taking his eyes off the road, and the two lapsed back into a meditative silence.

Chapter 10

My mind wandered back to the present as I drove through the small town of Junction. As I continued westward, steadily gaining altitude, the land began to change rapidly. I was now in the transitional area between the wetter Hill Country behind me, and the arid western part of the state still ahead. In the Austin area, as much as thirty inches of rain could fall in a year, but in the semi-arid regions of West Texas, total rainfall could be as little as ten inches. The transitional area was a region where the climate produced lush rainy seasons in some years, and year after year of heart-breaking drought at other times. It was primarily ranch country, the soil being too rocky and thin for farming. Mesquite trees and cactus were the most common plant life.

I passed through the two small ranching towns of Ozona and Sonora that together once served as the unofficial center of a thriving ranch culture in western Texas. The road followed wide avenues through residential areas with large Victorian-style homes languishing in the shade of hundred-year-old live oaks, streets that told of a more profitable time in Texas ranching. However, the road also traveled through deteriorating downtown areas that could not hide the decline in ranching fortunes in more recent years.

I had been driving for four hours and had traveled two hundred miles. It was almost one o'clock, and I realized that I was hungry. I stopped in Ozona at a Mexican restaurant. A square adobe building covered with stucco painted a garish orange, the restaurant was not hard to spot. I parked my truck in a gravel parking lot already crowded with pickup trucks, finding a place between an ancient Chevrolet truck filled with paint cans, ladders, and tarpaulins, and a newer Ford truck with "Sparky's Welding" written on the driver's side door. Entering the restaurant revealed an eclectic West Texas lunch crowd—working men such as from the painter's truck and the welding truck in soiled work clothes, oil field workers wearing their hard hats even to eat, ranchers in jeans and boots, and even a few white-collar types likely from local banks or insurance agencies. A harried waitress showed me to a table, dropped a menu and a glass of water on the table, and rushed off saying, "I'll be right back to get your order, sweetie."

Following a large and very good meal of green chile chicken enchiladas and several glasses of iced tea, I pulled back onto the highway and resumed my trip. Thoroughly enjoying the drive, I had almost forgotten about the hospital and the unpleasant issues awaiting me there. Cruising blissfully down the highway—alone in my mid-life crisis truck—I sang loudly and badly with the singers being broadcast by small radio stations in the remote towns.

As I cruised along singing, I began to climb into the high desert area of West Texas. Upon entering this region, the first thing I always noticed was a change in the shape of the mesas. In the wetter Hill Country the hills are rounded from erosion, but here the mesas are flat topped and sharp-edged. The rocks in the two areas are composed of exactly the same materials, but have eroded differently because of differences in rainfall. The flat-topped, sharp-edged mesas were the common landform in desert regions. What little plant life that survived tenuously on the flat tops and rocky slopes of the mesas consisted mainly of prickly pear, sotol, lechuguilla cacti, and the ever-present mesquite.

So much land is required to produce sufficient vegetation to feed a single cow or sheep here that ranching is unprofitable. The blessing of the land, however, was that it sat on huge deposits of oil and natural gas. The landscape was dotted with drilling rigs and pump stations.

I passed Fort Stockton, a small town built before the Civil War to hinder Indian raiding parties by denying them the water at the local springs. During frontier times this region had been the territory of the fearsome Comanches, who would hide in the mountains until going on extended raiding parties from Mexico almost to Colorado, often in times of a full moon. A full moon is still called a Comanche moon by many older people in this part of the country.

After Fort Stockton, still headed westward, I entered a region that is one of my favorite places to drive in. Although not beautiful in any traditional sense, the scenery was spectacular in its size and scope. Mostly flat desert terrain, the horizon was broken only by widely scattered distant mesas. The air was so free of pollution, and the sun so bright, that it was not uncommon upon topping even a small rise in the road to clearly see mesas twenty miles in the distance. Other than the scattered mesas, only an occasional windmill or oil drilling rig interrupted the immense emptiness of the landscape. The vistas were huge and overwhelming. A traveler has the impression that he can see forever, which is not a total exaggeration. I could already begin to see the Davis Mountains—my destination for the day—on the western skyline still some twenty miles away.

Just before reaching the mountains I passed through the small farming community of Balmorhea, an oasis in the West Texas desert. It was the location of a large natural rock swimming pool filled by natural springs. The spring water originated as rainfall in the mountains, filtered downhill through cracks and caverns in the limestone beds, and emerged cold and clear at the pool. In hot summer months, heat-weary Texans drove from all over the state to swim in the natural rock pool that ranged from a few feet deep to over twenty. For a moment I thought I could actually feel the chill of the cold water, sensory residue from many years before, and my mind began to drift back again.

Chapter 11

"Last one in the water is a rotten egg!" Charlie shouted as we began to emerge from Uncle Ray's old Chevrolet in the parking lot of the Balmorhea State Park swimming pool.

"Slow down. Slow down now," Uncle Ray said. "Everyone grab something before you go. Everyone has to carry something." He went to the rear of the car and opened the trunk.

"Hurry! Hurry," Roy Don said excitedly. "They're all going to beat us there." The "they" he was referring to were the kids who had ridden in the other car, the Cable family car. Charlie, Roy Don, Son, Dewayne, Billy Rex, and I had ridden with Uncle Ray. His own kids, Robert Earl, Aloe, and Blossom had ridden with Uncle Ben and my father in the other vehicle. Star, Crystal, and Sissy also rode in the other car.

After our fathers had come home from work Friday evening, the whole Alpine contingent of our family had piled into the family automobiles and driven from Alpine to a roadside park in the Davis Mountains. There were three entire families and Aunt Frances's two boys. There were twelve kids in all—all of us so excited we were about to burst. We had made camp at the park, cooked over an open fire, played, sung, and slept out under the stars. Today, Saturday, the three fathers had squeezed the twelve kids into two of the automobiles for the drive from our campground in the mountains to the swimming pool at Balmorhea Park.

At Uncle Ray's direction, we grabbed blankets, rubber tire inner tubes, and a hand pump from the back of the car. We raced to find an unoccupied shady spot under one of the huge cottonwood trees surrounding the pool. We spread our blankets on the grass and used the hand pump to frantically pump up the automobile tire inner tubes. At that time automobile tires still required rubber inner tubes to hold the air inside the harder outside shell of the tire. Flat tires were a frequent occurrence. When a tire went flat the tube was removed from the tire, the puncture located, and a patch applied to the leak. The tube was then put back into the tire, pumped up, and the tire put back on the car. This was repeated until a tube had been patched so many times that it was unsafe to continue to repair. Then a new inner tube would be purchased and used in the old tire, extending the life of the more expensive outer tire. The old tubes were not discarded, however. In many cases they were just beginning their useful life. Even if a tube had been patched so many times it was unsafe for a car, it was usually still usable as a swimming aid. An inner tube full of air would easily keep several kids afloat. We would cling to the sides of the tube while most of our body was in the water. We could play King of the Tube—several kids wrestling frantically in the water to climb on top of the tube while pushing others off—or one person could float blissfully sitting in the tube's center, their bottom in the cool water while their legs and upper torso projected over opposite sides of the tube.

When all the tubes had been inflated, the cousins raced in a wild, frantic charge to the cool water. The pool had a deep section, as much as twenty feet deep, and a large shallower area three to four feet deep, where the majority of us played, wrestled for tubes, rode on our fathers' shoulders, and tried to catch the thousands of minnows swimming between our legs.

"I'm the king of the tube!" Roy Don yelled as he climbed atop one of the larger tubes. Son dove under the water and came up under Roy Don's throne. He lifted one side of the tube out of the water and unceremoniously dumped the king into the water. He quickly assumed the throne and Charlie, Dewayne, and I immediately attacked him. The resulting flurry of kicking, screaming, laughing, and coughing up swallowed water dominated the shallower pool. The girls played a less rowdy version of the same game a short distance away.

By midafternoon we were exhausted, and my dad called us all out of the water. We lay on the blankets in the shade of a huge old cottonwood tree. Too excited to nap, we giggled and snickered and whispered confidences to the cousin next to us until the adults decided we were sufficiently rested. Uncle Ray herded the whole mob to the park concession stand and treated each of us to a soft drink and a snack. I copied Son and Charlie by asking for an RC Cola and a bag of peanuts. The drinks came in tall glass bottles. We drank a swallow or two and then poured the peanuts down the neck of the bottle into the cola. Each time we took a drink of the cola we would also get a mouthful of peanuts. It tasted better than filet mignon.

After our rest and snack, we were allowed to go back into the pool. Son and Roy Don had tired of fighting over the tubes. As the oldest, they were also best swimmers, and they began swimming on the opposite side of a cable stretched across the pool to mark where the water was deeper. They did not swim far on the deep side, but would go several strokes out before turning and coming back to the cable. Charlie, Dewayne, and I waded to the cable to watch. Charlie was a fairly accomplished swimmer, but Dewayne and I could still only swim a few feet with furious dog paddling.

"Want to see something scary?" Charlie asked.

"Sure," I said. "What?"

"Just go under here and look down into the deep end," Charlie instructed, and he took a deep breath and submerged while still holding the dividing cable with both hands.

I copied his action. Taking a breath, I let my feet slide out from under me forward and submerged. I looked forward and downward. The bottom sloped sharply downward starting immediately in front of where we were standing. The water got darker and darker as the pool deepened. Within a short distance I could no longer see the bottom, just a dark watery void. It looked like we were right on the edge of the end of the world, as if one step forward would send us tumbling into the abyss. It was dreadfully menacing. I recoiled in fear and tried to get back into the shallow water, but my feet slipped on the moss covered bottom, and I actually shifted forward. My feet slipped over the edge and downward. I still had a death grip on the wire cable, but I froze, unable to pull myself back. It was as if the deep, dark water was sucking me toward it. For what seemed an eternity I hung there frozen, bulging eyes locked on the terrifying darkness. Then I felt a hand grab the hair on the top of my head and pull me back into the shallow end and upright. I did not even notice the pain of being pulled by my hair. I found my footing and stood up out of the water, gasping for air, shivering in fear.

"You better be careful messing around in the deep water," Son scolded with genuine concern. He had pulled me back. "I don't know if I could pull you back if you got too far out there."

"See what I mean?" Charlie exclaimed. "Scary, isn't it? It looks like where the Creature from the Black Lagoon lives. It's spooky!"

"I heard there are catfish down at the bottom big enough to swallow a grown man," Roy Don said. "The only people that can go down there are scuba divers, and they carry spear guns for protection."

"You guys go play further back in the shallow water," Son admonished. We quickly moved away from the cable. I moved the fastest, having been truly shaken. I wanted to get as far as I could from the deep water. It was a long time after that before I ventured out of the shallow end of the pool.

Chapter 12

I experienced an involuntary shiver as I remembered the day I had stared into the deep water abyss. The physical act of the shiver woke me up—so to speak—from my memories of the pool. I left the small West Texas oasis behind and turned south on State Highway 17 toward the Davis Mountains.

The Davis Mountains were remnants of a vast volcanic field that at one time covered thousands of square miles in Texas and Northern Mexico. These rugged volcanic rocks gave the Davis Mountains a distinctive character, different from any other region in Texas or the United States.

Centuries of erosion and weathering of the lava flows created flat mesas that were columnar, jointed, with long, finger-like columns of lava rock exposed on the sides and slopes of the mountains. As these columns broke off and tumbled downhill, talus slopes of huge lava-rock boulders created some of the most rugged and spectacular mountains in the country.

As I climbed higher into the mountains, I rolled down the windows on my truck. The temperature was dropping noticeably. Vegetation became greener and more abundant as I followed the old Butterfield stagecoach route through a gap in the mountains called Wild Rose Pass. Frequent thunderstorms created by hot desert air rising rapidly into the mountains and meeting the cooler mountain air made for a greener environment than I had passed through in the desert below.

I entered a small valley divided by a meandering creek. In a grove of cottonwood and live oak trees beside the creek was a small roadside park. I pulled off the road and into the park. The park consisted of four distinct areas with concrete picnic tables, benches, and a fireplace at each. Memories of fireside wienie roasts and bedrolls under the stars began to play through my memory like a movie. This was the park where we had camped so many years ago.

✷✷✷✷✷

We had driven up from Alpine on Friday evening after work, all of the families loading their old automobiles with camping gear and caravanning to this park. My family, Uncle Ray's family, and the Cable family had come from Alpine; Henry and Frances from Pecos in the opposite direction. Each family took one of the picnic areas as their own campground, and we filled the small park with uncles, aunts, and cousins.

We laid tarpaulins on the ground to protect bedding laid on top of them, and another tarpaulin was used to cover the bedding in case it rained during the night. In my family's case, we made a single bed for all four of us. My mom and dad slept in the middle. I slept beside my father and Sissy slept beside my mother, the four of us snuggled under a single large quilt.

The delicious smell of my mother cooking eggs and bacon, and coffee boiling over an open fire, woke me in the morning. Even in summer, mornings in the mountains were chilly so I snuggled deeper in the warm bedroll next to my father. My father always tried to sleep late on Saturday morning, his recovery time after a week of hard physical work, while my mother got up to make breakfast.

Soon hunger and the happy squeals of other kids playing coaxed me from the bedroll. Wrapping a piece of toast around several pieces of bacon, I gulped down my breakfast. Sissy had also gotten up, and was eating cereal out of a cup.

"Come on," Dewayne said as he raced by with Billy Rex close behind. "We're going to play in the creek."

"Wait for us," I called after him. I swallowed the last of my toast and bacon and took off trailing them. Sissy followed behind. We joined the other cousins at the small creek that flowed just below the park.

We bounced from rock to rock along the stream that meandered through the valley, looking for frogs, lizards, fish, or anything else that would hold the interest of such a mob. The excited din of twelve kids playing with great vigor and joy could probably be heard for miles

"Snake! Get him!" I heard Charlie yell. I heard a frightened shriek from Aloe and saw Son, Roy Don, and Charlie throwing rocks at something near the bank of the creek. Aloe quickly retreated to the opposite bank where she was joined by Blossom and Robert Earl. Star and Crystal tried to get close to their brothers to see the snake. The boys had cornered a water moccasin.

"Don't get too close," Son warned.

Dewayne, Billy Rex, and I joined them in throwing rocks at the unfortunate reptile. We quickly stoned it to death.

Roy Don grabbed a broken tree branch off the bank and picked up the dead snake. He began to carry it around draped over the end of the stick. The girls screamed and recoiled in horror when Roy Don approached them with the dead serpent, while the boys, equally repulsed, tried to act brave and nonchalant. I desperately wanted to move away from the dead snake, but did not want my cousins to know I was afraid, so I tried to act as if I killed snakes every morning after breakfast and refused to shy away.

Suddenly, I was saved when a jackrabbit was flushed from the bushes near the creek. The rabbit bounded away rapidly.

"Get him!" Son yelled.

"Dinner!" Charlie said as he rapidly transitioned his attention from the snake to the rabbit. He began to chase the rabbit, and quickly the screaming cousins joined in hopeless pursuit of both him and the rabbit. Roy Don dropped the dead snake and joined in the chase. We would pursue the rabbit until something else grabbed our attention and diverted our chase. Meanwhile the adults were sitting around the fires drinking coffee, talking, reading, and sometimes napping. They could keep track of the kids by listening to our happy clamor.

By midday the sun was directly over the small valley, and it became quite warm. After a lunch of bologna sandwiches and Kool-Aid, the kids were loaded into the cars and we drove down from the mountains to Balmorhea State Park and its natural swimming pool. Several adults stayed behind to keep an eye on our possessions at the roadside park while the rest of us went swimming.

Late in the afternoon, the adults loaded the tired, sunburned kids back into the cars for the trip back up the mountains. In the evenings all the families normally shared a communal meal around a warming campfire. The kids roasted marshmallows and wieners on sticks. My father brought out his guitar, and Uncle Ben pulled out his harmonica. They struck up a tune and soon began singing old cowboy songs. I remember those as precious moments.

My father's family was a boisterous, argumentative bunch, however, and invariably a loud argument would break out among the uncles and aunts. When that happened the kids would just drift away to play quiet games or, exhausted, surrender to the beckoning warmth of our bedrolls.

When the argument started this night I drifted away and spotted Son Cable lying on his back on the hood of his family's old Chevy, looking at the stars. I climbed up and joined him.

"Whatcha doin'?" I asked.

"Trying to learn the stars," Son answered without looking away from the heavens.

"Why?"

"Because a cowboy knows where he is by reading the stars," Son explained. "When you're way out in the country you don't have roads and signs to guide you, so you have to be able to tell where you are by looking at the stars."

"Look," he said, "do you see the Big Dipper?"

I didn't so he carefully pointed it out for me. I was amazed that I actually could see a dipper outlined by stars.

"You use the Big Dipper to find the North Star," Son continued, and he showed me how to sight along the forward edge of the dipper to a bright star. He explained that this bright star was always in the north sky, even though the rest of the stars moved around in the sky. I didn't understand the moving part, but I did understand the North Star.

"You can always find the Big Dipper because it is so easy to see," Son explained, "and you can use it to find the North Star. If you can find the North Star you'll always know which direction you're going."

It was one of those memories that sticks with you all your life. I never forgot his patient lesson, and I've always known what direction I was traveling at night, thanks to the simple cowboy logic of twelve-year-old Son Cable.

Chapter 13

The two travelers from the Panhandle were passing through Pecos, a small, dusty farming town. They had turned onto Interstate 10, the main east-west artery across Texas after finally getting out of the Panhandle, and followed it westward to Pecos. The freeway allowed them to avoid most of the town as it hurried on west to El Paso. Just outside Pecos, the two turned off the freeway onto a smaller state highway heading southwest toward Balmorhea, the Davis Mountains, and ultimately Alpine, though that was still over one hundred fifty miles away.

The land southwest of Pecos was flat and featureless, part of what was once a vast cotton-farming region that made landowners rich before irrigation used up the ground water and turned the area into an almost unusable dessert. As the travelers drove they passed fallow fields, falling-down houses, and rusty farm equipment. They turned down a dirt road that showed no sign of use, and pulled behind an abandoned farmhouse to stop and fill the gas tank from the cans of gasoline in the truck. The men took time to eat sandwiches they had packed the night before, washed down with soft drinks from a cooler in the back seat.

"Damn," the older of the two said as he looked around. "I always thought the Panhandle was ugly, but this area makes it look downright attractive. This is some butt-ugly country."

"Looks like it might have done okay at some time from the look of these old houses and rusted-out equipment," the other man said, "but it sure as hell has reached the end of its rope now." The man crushed the empty soft drink can he had just drained and placed it in a sack they had carried for refuse behind the passenger seat, then walked around the truck to the driver's side.

"I'll drive awhile. You get some rest," he said, as the other man got into the passenger seat. The younger man pulled the truck back onto the highway and headed southwest toward the Davis Mountains in the distance.

"Keep an eye out for a good place to pull over and spend the night," the passenger said after they had driven a few miles. "It's getting late. We won't get there before dark, so we'd probably be better off finding a place to sleep somewhere short of there."

Chapter 14

The roar of a large diesel truck barreling by on the highway next to the roadside park startled me back to real time. Reluctantly leaving my memories, I pulled my truck back onto the highway and soon arrived in the small mountain town of Fort Davis. Fort Davis was another of the forts built to protect the stagecoach route and settlers from Indian raids, an effort that was mostly ineffective. In addition to the Comanches, the Mescalero Apaches also called the Davis Mountains home. The army had never been particularly effective against either tribe.

The old fort had been restored, and appeared ready to be moved into and used. Fort Davis was thriving as a tourist destination, and Texans wanting second homes out of the desert heat were eagerly subdividing and developing any land that could be acquired in the area. Known as the Highest Town in Texas, Fort Davis has an elevation of over five thousand feet. I had climbed forty-five hundred feet while driving west this day. Just the high-altitude coolness of the late afternoon fall air would have made the trip worthwhile, I thought.

Turning off the main highway, I traveled up a smaller, winding road to the Davis Mountains State Park, a few miles outside town, the site of Indian Lodge. Indian Lodge was a landmark in West Texas. It was built during the Depression as a Civilian Conservation Corps (CCC) project, employing destitute men from all over Texas. Much of the core structure built by those men still remained. The lodge was built to resemble the Indian pueblo villages in nearby New Mexico and Arizona. Built at the end of the valley, high up on the sides of the mountains closing the rear of the valley, huge cliffs towering above the lodge, the whitewashed stucco walls glowed in the last direct sunlight as I arrived and checked in.

Following dinner in the lodge restaurant, I wandered into the great hall, still furnished with hand carved cedar furniture made during the Depression. Two huge rock fireplaces anchored the opposite ends of the great room. Above the mantle of the nearest fireplace hung a large framed photograph. It was a posed group picture of about two hundred of the men who worked on the construction of the lodge. Written at the bottom of the picture was "CCC Co. 879, May 7, 1934." I looked at the back row, just right of center, and stared into the very young face of my now deceased father.

It had been twenty years since I'd last been to this room and seen this photograph, but I had no trouble locating my father. He appeared thin, almost gaunt. He looked so much younger than the other men that he seemed out of place. He had been sixteen years old when the picture was taken. The other workers looked old enough to have children of their own that age. I found myself wondering what he had been thinking when the picture was taken. Was he relieved just to have a job, a place to sleep, and food to eat? Had he ever wondered about what the future might hold for him? Was he lonely, away from his family and on his own at that young age? I found it impossible to imagine what it must have been like. Trying to look back almost seventy years and read some emotion into my young father's expression, the only thing I could think of was relief.

Pulling away from the picture, I wandered outside onto a large porch. The porch opened to a view of the valley back toward Fort Davis. The fading sunset colored the few clouds pink and purple, and darkness had already absorbed the eastern sky. I sat in an ancient wooden rocking chair to enjoy the beautiful Texas sunset. Gently rocking back and forth, I thought more about my father.

My father had been one of eight children. His father—my grandfather—worked on construction sites all across Texas. His mother had died shortly after my father was born. Grandfather had to travel to other parts of the state for construction projects, which forced him to put his children into foster homes. He paid the foster families to care for the kids while he traveled.

My father had told me almost nothing about his life then. It had only been through tearful remembrances of his two surviving siblings that I had learned of the ugliness of their existence in foster care. I came to understand that he never talked about it because he did not want to remember.

During the Great Depression in rural Texas, almost everyone was struggling to survive. The farm and ranch families with whom my father and his siblings were placed used them essentially as slave labor. And worse. Whispers of sexual abuse of his sister, who was a very attractive teenager at the time, had circulated in the family for years. When Grandfather had come for visits the kids were cleaned up, put into new clothes, and threatened with beatings if they told of the mistreatment they had suffered. If Grandfather had any idea what was really going on—and I find it hard to believe he didn't have suspicions—he chose to ignore it. The simple truth was that times were hard and people had to sacrifice in many ways to survive. The kids could not live with him at construction sites, and he had to earn the money for the family to survive. I believed he *chose* not to know—that he chose to *survive*.

When my father was thirteen and his brother Ray was fifteen, unable to tolerate the abuse any longer, they ran away. They hitchhiked and rode empty railroad cars far into West Texas. Near starvation and desperate, they had the good fortune to come upon a rancher so in need of cheap labor that he was willing to hire two greenhorn kids. Neither of them ever went back to school. They became cowboys, and they loved it—riding horses, working cattle, and the freedom of the cowboy life. My father often said that he had never since been as happy as when he was a young man working as a cowboy.

World War II started soon after he married my mother, and he was drafted into the army. As an uneducated cowboy working on remote ranches, I suspected my father was barely, if at all, aware of what the conflict was about. Nonetheless, he served during World War II and came home afterward to a changed Texas. An economic and cultural transition had taken place while he had been away. Continuing a decline in fortunes that began during the Depression, by the end of the war the large Texas ranches had all but ceased to exist as viable economic entities. The ranch culture and the time of the itinerant cowboy had passed into Texas mythology. My father came back from the war to discover that no one needed or wanted cowboys. He had to move into town and find other work. He ultimately followed his own father into construction, finding work as a carpenter, but he never got over being a cowboy. Until the day he died, he saw himself as a cowboy forced into temporary city employment, just waiting for the right opportunity to go back to what he really loved.

Stars began to appear in the darkening sky as I sat alone on the patio, thinking about my father's mostly unhappy life. Slowly rocking, I looked up and was momentarily surprised at the brightness of the stars. I had forgotten how bright the stars appeared in the low light and low pollution levels of West Texas. Easily locating the Big Dipper, I used the methodology Son Cable had taught me so many years before to find the North Star and determined that I would be heading south in the morning to go to his funeral.

Chapter 15

The two travelers were tired and looking for a place to stop and sleep.

"How about that little roadside park we just passed?" the older man, who was still riding passenger, said as he noticed a small park on the edge of their headlights' illumination. "It looked like it had several campsites. Maybe one of them will be isolated some."

"Good idea," the driver said as he braked. They pulled off the road and made a U-turn, then drove back to the small park. There was no other traffic on the road through the mountains this late at night. There was a full moon and millions of stars which allowed the men to see plainly even after they turned off the truck's lights.

There were several small campsites, each with a concrete cooking pit and concrete tables and benches. Limbs from large cottonwood and live oak trees provided a canopy over the camping area. A small stream passed under a bridge on the highway and meandered past the small park. The two men got out of their truck and walked about to stretch tired muscles, and stopped to relieve themselves near the creek.

"Pretty little place, isn't it?" the older man remarked.

"Yeah," the other replied, "the kind of place I would have loved as a kid." He was unaware that this was the park where the Cable and Carter families had camped, and the kids had played so vigorously many years previous, and that Tom Carter had parked there this very afternoon to remember those trips.

The two men sat on a large rock by the little creek, listening to the water chatter by. They remembered and talked about camping trips they had taken as children.

"Did you ever imagine we would be going on a trip like this to do what we're going to do?" the younger man asked. "I mean back then, when we were little."

"No. I sure did not," the older one sighed.

"How much further you reckon we got to go?" the younger man asked.

"I'd say Alpine is about an hour off," the older one replied. "We better get some sleep. You stretch out across the back seat and I'll take the front." And the two walked back to their truck, parked in almost the exact spot where Son Cable had delivered his North Star lesson from the hood of his old family car.

"Tom, I'm starting to get really concerned. The protest by the OB/GYN physicians seems to be gathering support," was the recorded warning from Robert Blake. Before pulling out of the Indian Lodge parking lot Friday morning, I had used my cell phone to check voice mail at the hospital in Austin. Blake's message continued, "I'm getting requests from more and more doctors in the department wanting to attend the meeting to support the request. An ugly discussion of the issue has been taking place in the physicians' lounge. I was afraid refusing to let them attend would just fuel the fire, so I granted permission for all interested physicians to attend the board meeting."

In fact, it would have been quite acceptable for him to decline the request. The boardroom was relatively small, so the meetings were open to participants and invited guests only. I frequently rejected requests to attend. Blake knew that by the time I got to the hospital on Monday morning it would be too late for me to reverse his decision. I had no doubt that he wanted to leave the board with the impression that physician dissatisfaction was rampant. Even if I stopped the physicians from attending, Blake would still come off as more physician-friendly. I had to admit that he had played this well.

A second message was from Dr. Kerley, proclaiming his anger at my canceling his meeting, and attempting to use the controversy involving the OB/GYN physicians to his own advantage.

"Canceling our meeting at that late hour," he complained, "was simply unacceptable, particularly when I know that you had just met with doctors Howard and Fine. Now, I have never gotten involved in the politics involving the women's center, and I do not wish to do so now, but if you do not show me more professional courtesy, I may have to join that group."

Clearly a threat—he hoped I would approve his mega-million dollar machine to prevent his aligning with doctors Howard and Fine.

By the time I finished listening to the messages, most of the mellow mood I had acquired since leaving Austin had vanished. I was tense and angry as I pulled out onto the road for the short trip to Alpine. However, unlike days in the hospital, as I resumed driving I could almost physically feel the concern falling away from me. As I relaxed, I began to lose myself once more in the beauty of the mountains and the music on the radio. The hostile messages soon became a vague memory.

I once again passed through clusters of huge volcanic mountains, separated by wide grassy valleys. As I approached Alpine, the mountains became fewer and separated by wider valleys. Some of the mountains were spectacular, however. One such was Mitre Peak, a sharply pointed peak that towered some fifteen hundred feet above the road and resembled the nose cone of a giant rocket sticking out of the earth. Local legend claims that it was named for its resemblance to a bishop's mitre hat.

By ten o'clock I arrived in Alpine, one of the prettiest small towns in Texas. Located along Alpine Creek in the Alpine Valley, it was the northeastern boundary and the county seat of Brewster County, the largest county within the state of Texas. The land was an eclectic display of large, rugged mountains, high plateaus, and broad valleys separated by gently sloping intermountain plains. To the south of Alpine, toward Mexico, the country becomes rugged desert mountains, where temperatures often reached 115 degrees in the summer months. Alpine, however, was located at a higher elevation with a much milder climate. Alpine Valley was at an elevation of 4,484 feet, while some of the peaks surrounding the valley rose to six and seven thousand feet. Alpine Valley creased the mountains from east to west.

Directly to the south of the town, facing me as I drove in, was A Mountain. The mountain got its name from rocks arranged into the shape of a fifty-foot "A." Those stacked rocks were painted white, making the huge "A" visible for miles, and creating an easily identifiable landmark for the town.

To the east was a similar mountain, except that the painted rocks on this mountain created the monogram "SR." This identified Sul Ross State University, the small college built on the side of the mountain. Sul Ross trained primarily school teachers, but also had a very good agriculture program reflective of the ranching in the region, and was the only school in America where a student could study to be a farrier, someone who shoes horses. It was a campus where almost everyone wore jeans and boots, and cowboy hats were the most common headgear.

Westward, on the opposite end of Alpine Valley, stood two almost identical mountains known as Twin Peaks. The two mountains resembled the breasts of two women lying side by side. A local Indian legend told of two maidens who fought bitterly over the same brave man. The Great Spirit became so annoyed with their fighting that he turned them into two mountains, forcing them to lie together for eternity. The peaks were originally called Twin Sisters Peaks, but more modest Alpine citizens did not feel comfortable with attention called to the peaks' similarity to female breasts, and the name was shortened to Twin Peaks. The Cable house where I had played as a small child was on the west side of town, toward the Twin Peaks, and I understood that Son Cable had bought a place somewhere even west of that, at the very base of the two mountains.

Alpine had been the completion point of the final segment of the transcontinental Southern Pacific Railroad, in the middle of one of the last open grazing land areas of Texas. It was one of the few places in the United States where the ranching culture had survived, and where a ranch of less than a hundred thousand acres was considered a small spread. Fewer than seven thousand people lived in Alpine, not counting the two thousand college students. Although beautiful, the town was remote and isolated, almost two hundred miles from another city of any size, the nearest being El Paso to the west. Its remoteness kept Alpine small and most of the locals liked it that way.

The city was divided by the railroad tracks running through town east and west. Holland Avenue, the unofficial main street, paralleled the railroad tracks, and was the location of the downtown commercial district. The remainder of the city consisted of wide, tree-lined residential streets fronted by one-story homes, most with wide covered porches extending in a friendly invitation toward the street.

Driving directly to the funeral home, I parked in the parking lot, took a deep breath in preparation, and walked to the two-story cream-colored stucco building on the corner. I pulled open the ornate, heavy carved wooden door and went inside.

The lobby just inside the door was cool and dark, with a viewing room off to the side. At the front of the viewing room, resting on a stand about waist high, was a coffin containing Son Cable's body.

The coffin was not a modern one. It was a simple wooden box of unfinished pine lumber. The top of the coffin had been taken off and was leaned against the wall, exposing the body from head to boots. Several floral arrangements had been placed around the coffin. Son was dressed in neatly pressed jeans and a new white shirt. He was wearing his worn but polished cowboy boots, and a western string tie. A white cowboy hat lay atop his chest. I remembered Aunt Frances saying that this would be a cowboy funeral. The simple, hand-made coffin and Son's attire fit that description.

Reluctantly sitting down on the front row, it took me several minutes to actually look at Son's face. I first studied the room, the chairs, the coffin, and finally, when I had run out of other things to look at, I looked at Son

Cable. My stomach felt like it had suddenly been filled with helium, creating an unsettling lightness. Gradually the feeling subsided, and I studied Son's face. He was, or had been, only four years my senior, but a lifetime of hard work in the elements had aged him beyond his years. The sandy hair had receded, leaving a lot of forehead visible. He was still thin, almost gaunt, and his hands showed evidence of abuse from years of working with tools and ropes. He did not look used up, I thought to myself, but he did look well used. I thought how different I would appear in that box, in a business suit, after years of working in an air-conditioned office.

Before long I was lost in thought, losing track of time. I thought about Son as a boy, and of how little I knew of him as a man. I wondered what his life had been like. "Were you happy?" I asked him, or imagined that I did. "Were you happy with what you did with your life?" Son did not answer.

As I sat looking at him I began to see him through a child's eyes. I saw us doing the things that had delighted us nearly a half century earlier. I remembered again our soap box derby races, and the day I had won. I thought about the trip back to the house that day, and remembered that we would have passed our old lizard graveyards. At that time West Texas was literally crawling with lizards, small green and black striped lizards, six or seven inches long. The lizards zipped here and there across the hot dirt, pausing to lift two legs to cool their feet, then the other two, and then off again in search of insects and ants. When there was nothing else to do, we would entertain ourselves for hours hunting lizards, bagging them with slingshots or BB guns. At the end of the day we would proudly haul in our kill, sometimes as many as two-dozen lizards.

Lizard bodies attracted ants like crazy so leaving them lying around the house was not an option, and our parents did not like us throwing them in the trash for the same reason, so we decided to bury them. One of the cousins came up with the idea of creating lizard graveyards. We loved it! The graves were made by scooping out a small trench with a spoon and inserting a lizard, then taking two twigs and tying them into a cross with string or thread, which we then placed at the head of the lizard grave. We placed the graves in a straight line, then another matching line, then into larger squares of graves, all with tiny crosses. We even created walls by stacking stones around the tiny graveyards to mark the boundaries. We eventually had lizard graveyards in the pasture behind the house as large as twenty square feet.

Then, as kids do, we lost interest and went on to something else, leaving the tiny graves to wind and rain erosion, and time. Many years later, when I remembered the lizard graveyards, I wondered what a team of archaeologists, thousands of years from now, would think if they discovered one of those long forgotten lizard graveyards—probably that they had discovered a long lost society of Christian lizards who buried their dead in cemeteries like humans. Can you imagine that discussion?

While we were recovering from one of our soap box derby races, Dewayne came up with the idea of the Great Horny Toad Chariot Race. In addition to lizards, there was an abundance of horned lizards or horned toads, which we called horny toads, running around the area. About the size of the palm of an adult hand, horned toads were more or less round and covered on their backside and head with thorn-like projections, which everyone called horns. The small beasts looked ferocious, but were more or less harmless. They survived mainly by eating ants. When frightened, they puffed up and squeezed a stream of a dark liquid, labeled tobacco juice by the locals, out of one of their eyes. A horned toad could be put to sleep by turning it upside down and rubbing its belly, a pastime we never grew tired off. We would catch the poor creatures, flip them on their back, and stroke till they fell sleep. Then we would release them and start over.

Dewayne had seen a movie with chariot races. "What if we make chariots out of matchboxes?" he asked one day. "We could use wheels from all the broken toy cars. We could hitch the chariots to horny toads, and have a race."

"Cool!" Robert Earl exclaimed.

"That's a good idea," Roy Don agreed.

"Let's do it," Son said, and the Great Horny Toad Chariot Race was on.

It was a doomed idea from the start. It never occurred to any of us that a horned toad would not follow a prescribed race course. We spent days capturing horned toads and making chariots and string harnesses. When the day of the big race arrived even the girl cousins came to watch the grand spectacle. We each put our racing toad at the starting line and released them simultaneously when Son hollered, "Go!"

The seven toads immediately took off in seven different directions.

"Eeeeeeeek!" screamed the terrified girls as the out-of-control chariot racing toads ran between their legs. The girls panicked and ran in whichever direction they were pointed at the time, stomping their feet. Most of the unfortunate racing toads were killed within a matter of seconds, squished. The few survivors raced off into the prairie dragging our matchbox chariots behind them.

Following the ill-planned race we buried the squished racing toads with honor and great solemnity in one of the lizard graveyards. None of the toads that escaped into the prairie were ever found.

We also loved going to the movies that summer. On Saturdays we usually went as a group to the small movie theatre in downtown Alpine. We would see a feature, a cartoon, and a serial cliffhanger, all for an admission price of twelve cents each. Popcorn was ten cents a box. If our parents couldn't supply the money for the Saturday movie, we could raise it by finding and selling six soda bottles for four cents apiece. All soft drinks came in bottles then, and people often discarded them in spite of their redemption value. There were plenty around. Twelve kids scrounging for a week could easily find more than enough soda bottles to provide movie money. We even maintained a bank of extra bottles to draw from if the current week's pickings were too slim. As the oldest, Son was in charge of the bank, withdrawing however many bottles were needed to provide movie tickets for all, and resisting our pleas to withdraw bottles from the bank to buy more soda and candy during the week. Son insisted that our bank was a movie bank only, and no amount of pleading would persuade him to waste bottles on anything else. Probably because of his careful control, the gang of cousins went to the movies just about every Saturday.

Usually the movies were westerns with singing cowboys, like Roy Rogers and Gene Autrey. My personal favorite cowboy actor was Lash LaRue, a cowboy hero dressed all in black who used a bullwhip to lash guns out of the hands of outlaws before the bad guys could draw and fire. Lash was also Son's favorite, and the two of us would practice our whipping skills with makeshift whips of cotton rope tied to a stick handle, imagining ourselves to be whipping the pistols from the hands of bad outlaws. Mostly we just made welts on our own arms and legs.

But going to the movies only filled one day a week. The rest of the week we had to provide our own entertainment, and somehow we filled every day with new adventures. Some of the play was dangerous, and we were lucky that no one was ever seriously injured. The closest we came to a disaster was the Chief Blister Head episode.

During a frantic game of cowboys and Indians we came upon a discarded bucket of tar at a construction site. We amused ourselves by poking sticks into the sticky goo for a while, until Roy Don pulled a large glob out on the end of a stick.

"I wonder if this stuff will burn," Roy Don said. We were forbidden to play with matches, but one of us always had a few. Roy Don pulled a match from his pocket, struck it, and held it to the glob of tar stuck to the end of the stick. We were amazed to see the tar easily ignite into a steady flame. Roy Don started to dance around, waving the torch over his head like we'd seen Indians do in the cowboy movies.

"Woo woo woo woo!" he cried, patting his free hand against his mouth to make the savage chant we had seen in western movies. The rest of us fell in behind him in an impromptu Indian line dance to celebrate the deaths of all the settlers we would soon be scalping.

We danced through the construction site whooping and hollering, Roy Don leading the way with the torch above his head. Everything was fine until the fire began to melt the tar. Suddenly a large, burning blob of tar dropped off the stick and landed smack on top of Roy Don's head. For a moment Roy Don kept dancing on as the rest of us stopped in shock at the sight of the top of his head igniting in flame. When the heat of burning, melting tar reached his scalp, he let out a loud scream and threw away the torch. He began beating at the flame on top of his head with his hands but only succeeded in mashing the burning tar further into his hair and spreading it into a wider burning surface.

For a moment the rest of us were too shocked to move. Then Son leapt into action to save his younger brother.

"Dirt!" he yelled. "Dirt will put out a fire!" His father had taught him to pile dirt on a campfire to put it out without wasting water in a dry country.

The rest of us immediately began to scoop up handfuls of dirt, which we threw on Roy Don's head. For a few moments it appeared a dust storm had sprung up on the prairie.

"That's enough! Stop!" Son finally yelled, and we did.

As the air cleared, we could see a human dirt ball sitting on the ground crying loudly. A thin wisp of smoke curled out of the large pile of dirt on top of his head. He was so dirty that the only things recognizable were his eyes and mouth.

Roy Don, probably more terrified by our trying to bury him alive than the fire on his head, continued to wail. Son picked him up off the ground and tried to brush off the dirt, then led him back to the house.

Fortunately, Roy Don was not seriously hurt. His parents had to shave his head to get the tar off. He had a large, angry blister on the very top of his bald head, and after the rest of us got over being scared, we started calling Roy Don Chief Blister Head.

I was chuckling to myself as I sat in the funeral home remembering Chief Blister Head when I was startled by a slap on my back and a loud, "Hello Cuz!"

Chapter 17

"Hello Cuz!" the man slapping me on the back said cheerfully as he sat down next to me. "Man it's good to see you, even under these circumstances."

It was Billy Rex. He was approaching fifty now, a successful banker in a small Hill Country town. His thin blond hair was turning gray. He still wore the thick eyeglasses he'd worn most of his life, and at five foot ten, Billy Rex was showing some middle-aged banker's thickening. He was now a confident, gentle man, a far cry from the shy, bespectacled kid of that long ago summer.

"Hello, Billy Rex!" I said as I shook his hand. "Good to see you too."

After a burst of greetings and family information swapping, we lapsed into silence as we sat in the funeral parlor with Son, each of us lost in our own memories of the man, but mostly of the boy. Other visitors came, paid their respects, and left, but we stayed on.

At noon we heard church bells around town signaling the hour. Billy Rex and I got up from our chairs and walked outside into what had become a beautiful fall day; bright sunlight and only thin, wispy clouds scattered in a very blue sky. We both climbed into my truck and drove uphill toward Sul Ross, where Billy Rex and I both had graduated. We spent an hour eating lunch at a small café we had remembered from our college days.

"Let's drive around Alpine a little to see what's changed," Billy Rex suggested.

"Good idea," I said, and we headed back into Alpine proper. We visited some of our youthful haunts, and eventually found ourselves at the small house outside town my family had rented during that summer.

"Goddamn! This is depressing," I said as we arrived.

It was apparent that the house had been unoccupied for many years, and it showed the detrimental effects of time and neglect. Weeds grew waist high outside of the house and erupted through broken boards on the porch. Large chunks of stucco had fallen off the sides of the house. All of the windows were broken or missing, as were the doors. There was a sag in the roof that left the middle several feet lower than the ends. The windmill I had loved so much was gone, as was the tank that had accompanied it. Two vehicles, an old Chevrolet automobile and an ancient Ford pickup, had been abandoned in the weeds. The windows were broken out of the rusting hulks and the tires were missing, the vehicles sitting on wheels sunken into the earth. A mean-looking cur dog barked at us threateningly from the weeds in front of the house. It was sad to see a place I remembered so fondly so run down.

I did not get out of the truck. The incessantly barking dog discouraged any closer inspection, but from the street I could see into what had been the living room where I'd laid on the floor at my father's feet listening to the radio. As I sat there remembering, I could almost hear the *Fibber McGee and Molly* show and my father's laughter.

My sister and I would lie on the floor while our parents sat listening to the voice on the radio, picturing vividly the unimaginable clutter of Fibber McGee's closet or the majestic beauty of Gene Autry's Flying A ranch. Nothing I have ever seen on TV matched the beauty of the scenes I imagined while listening to the radio.

"Hey Cuz, we'd better get going now," Billy Rex said, softly. I had been lost in thought, not sure how long I had sat staring into the house.

"Yeah. You're right," I said. For the first time since receiving the call about Son's death and starting on this trip, I was beginning to feel a real sense of loss.

Billy Rex and I both were quiet as we drove back toward the funeral home to retrieve his car. I suddenly remembered driving home with my father at night after some trip to Fort Stockton. I had lain across the front seat with my head in my father's lap as he drove us home. It had been dark in the car except for the glow from the instrument panel on the dash. We had no radio or air conditioning in the car, so the only sounds were the tires humming on the road which I felt more than heard, and the rush of air as we drove with the windows down—the poor man's air conditioning. My whole world was reduced to the space from the dash to my father's lap, dimly lit by the glow from the dash lights, surrounded by rushing air, small and safe. I had fantasized about being a tiny person climbing among the wires under the dash in the glowing dim lights, and soon fell asleep and woke up at home. I can't remember ever feeling as safe as I did then. Even now, as a grown man, there are days when I wish I could once more retreat to the safe cocoon of my father's lap on that trip.

Chapter 18

After dropping Billy Rex off at his car, I was suddenly lonely. Going nowhere in particular, I drove west toward Twin Peaks. After a few minutes of allowing my mind to simply follow my hood ornament down the street, I glanced off to the right, and several tall metal poles supporting banks of lights towering above the one-story houses captured my attention. It was the high school football stadium, and I turned my truck toward it out of curiosity.

Approaching the light towers, I saw the football field, turning brown from overuse and weather, flanked by wood and steel grandstands painted gray and silver. The stands on the near side of the stadium were larger, and supported a square, windowed press box above the last row of seats. On the end of the field closest to the road was a broad one-story cinder-block building with a flat roof. This building contained dressing rooms and weight training facilities for the home team, the Alpine Bucks. An eight-foot-high chain-link fence surrounded the entire stadium complex.

A wide gate in the fence behind the field house was open, and several pickup trucks were parked inside. I coasted to a spot among the trucks and parked. Getting out slowly, I stretched, and walked around the right side of the field house. At the front of the building was a grassy, open area between the field house and the towering metal goalposts. In the middle of that open space, a very large man was hitting golf balls toward the far end of the football field. Another man sat in a lawn chair off to the side beneath a large green and white beach umbrella. A plastic cooler sat on the ground next to him. He pulled a can of beer from the cooler just as I rounded the corner. Between the two men scattered golf balls waited their turn to be struck.

The two men were almost identically dressed. They wore gray spandex shorts and gray tee shirts with ALPINE BUCKS printed across the front in purple block letters. Both wore black rubber-soled athletic shoes and calf-high white athletic socks. The man hitting golf balls wore a purple baseball cap with a large gold A on the front. The man watching wore a cap made of camouflage colors. Neither had noticed me. I watched silently as the large man pounded several balls into a high arch toward the goalposts at the far end of the field.

"I guess I've seen a worse golf swing, but not by a human being," I announced loudly as I strolled toward the two men.

Both heads swiveled toward me. A wide grin spread across the face of the man in the chair. The larger man looked at me with surprise for a moment, and then replied, "Well if you've seen a better swing it sure as hell wasn't in the mirror!"

"Holy moly!" said the first man to the other in a scolding tone. "Did you forget to lock the gate again? Now look what's gotten in!" He rose to meet me as I approached. "God-all-Mighty! Where did you come from?"

Pecos Cook, slightly larger than average size, still moved with the athletic grace of his youth. Though in his fifties, he still looked as muscular as when we three had played football together at Sul Ross, nearly thirty years earlier. At six feet tall he appeared to still be very close to his playing weight of 180 pounds. What had once been black hair showed mostly gray sticking out from under the camouflage cap, however, and heavy lines around his eyes told a different tale than his build. He had a wide, flat, deeply tanned face, almost Indian in appearance.

"Damn it's good to see you Pecos," I exclaimed as I grabbed his outstretched hand. Pecos was not a nickname. His parents had actually named him after the famous West Texas landmark river.

The larger man, Frank "Pudgie" Bowen had been six feet four and 230 pounds in his playing days. Now however, he looked to weigh over 300 pounds. In college he'd shaved his head—a skinhead before his time—but now, as he removed his cap to wipe his brow, he appeared totally bald. Looking like a huge bear walking upright, he approached me with arms held wide and gripped me in a hug that almost knocked the wind from me.

"Toes!" he exclaimed enthusiastically.

My college nickname had been Twinkle-toes, from a cartoon character—a large clumsy football player—in beer commercials. Over time, Twinkle had been dropped, and I became just Toes.

After several minutes of handshakes, hugs, and backslaps, Pecos fetched two more lawn chairs and the three of us settled around the ice chest. Pudgie fetched beers from the chest for all of us.

"What in God's name are you doing in Alpine, Toes?" asked Pecos.

"I came for Son Cable's funeral," I answered after a drink from the cold beer can.

"That's right," Pudgie said, his mood suddenly more somber. "I'd forgotten that you were kin to him. Cousins, wasn't it?"

"Yeah." I swallowed some more beer. "We were cousins. Close as kids, but I haven't seen him much in the last few years. I felt like I needed to come to the funeral though."

"I'd heard that Son died," replied Pecos. "Too bad. He was a good man."

"I didn't know you even knew Son," I said with surprise.

"This is Alpine, Toes," he answered. "Everyone knows everyone here. You been livin' in the big city too long. Still runnin' hospitals?"

"Yeah, or at least I was when I left Austin. Never know what'll be there when I get back."

"You havin' trouble?" Pudgie asked as he took a long draw on his beer.

"No more than normal," I answered. I followed his example and took a long cold drink. "It's hard to believe now that job security was one reason I left coaching and went into health care. Now hospital administrators get fired more often than last-place baseball managers."

"Well maybe," Pudgie said slyly, "you need to come back to coaching. I'm sure the company is better."

"That may not be so far-fetched," I told him, "but for now, I'm here for a funeral."

"That might be a subject for more beers than we have available," added Pecos. "But we can always go get more."

"No," I said, laughing, "let's leave that one for another time. Are you giving Pudgie golf lessons?"

"Trying, but it's like trying to teach water ballet to an armadillo."

"I resemble that!" Pudgie whined as he reached for another beer.

"Why aren't you getting ready for a football game?" I asked. "This is Friday isn't it?"

Pecos said, "We have an open date this week, so we gave the kids the day off. We thought we'd see if there was any hope of resuscitating Pudgie's golf game, but after watching awhile, I think it's time to call Dr. Kervorkian."

"We'll see about that," Pudgie snorted. "With Toes here we have a foursome."

"Foursome? You teaching math now?" I inquired. "I only count three."

Pudgie just pointed to a place behind where I sat. I turned and saw a third man coming from the field house, buckling his belt. Looking up he noticed me and hesitated, and then recognition registered on his face.

"Are there no standards at all around this place?" the man complained, feigning exasperation. "I just excused myself for a minute to take a Twinkle-toes, and you two manage to lower the collective IQ before I can get my pants back up!"

"Pig!" I shouted gleefully. "I don't believe it! What are you doing here? I thought you went into administration. Are the commodes in administration too small for your big ass?"

"I come over here for the dirty magazines these two moral reprobates hide in their desks. How in the world are you doing, Toes?"

Shorter than Pecos and Pudgie at about five feet ten inches, Paul Peterson had been a fearless 175-pound defensive back in college. Blond then, he was mostly gray now, but he still wore the sixties throwback flattop haircut. Paul had a turned-up nose that allowed someone talking to him to look into his nostrils. Someone on the team had remarked that it reminded him of a pig's snout, and Paul became "Pig" Peterson. He had put on weight, not to the degree that Pudgie exhibited, but a beer gut preceded him as he walked toward me. He had clear blue eyes that were now focused through wire-framed glasses. Pig also had coached football for several years after college, but twenty years later had moved into school administration. He was Alpine's high school principal now.

"I'm doing fine for an old fart, Pig," I replied, and the two of us went through the handshake and back-slapping ritual as I answered the same questions I had answered for Pecos and Pudgie.

"Well, I came to play golf and win money," announced Pig, "and I have a parent-teacher meeting tonight, so let's get with it."

"Play golf? Are you guys going over to the golf course?" I asked.

"Oh no," explained Pecos. "We're going to play men's golf. None of that sissy stuff for us on a grass course with flat greens!"

"Well since I am without question the best golfer in this crowd," said Pig, "and since Toes has never played the course, I'll take him as my partner. We'll play Pecos and Pudgie for the free and clear title to Brewster County."

"Wait a minute," I said, "where are we playing?"

"Right here." Pudgie answered. "We start right here, go under the home stands, through the far goalposts, back under the visitors' stands, and back to this spot. We'll designate this chair as the home hole. First team to get both their players back to this chair, and you have to hit the chair, wins.

"And you only get to use one club," he added, "and if you have an unplayable lie you have to retreat at least fifty paces and take a five-stroke penalty."

With that, he let out a cackling laugh that I remembered instantly from college. Any time any mischief had occurred that cackle would invariably be heard retreating into the distance.

After we had all chosen a club from the bag, Pecos said, "I'll go first to show you girls the way." He dropped a ball on a patch of good grass, and with all the seriousness of Arnold Palmer teeing off at the US Open, he took a soft swing and launched the ball toward the home stands. His ball took a couple of crazy bounces when it landed and rolled to a stop close to the grandstands, in perfect alignment to go underneath them on his next shot.

"Wow! Good shot!" Pig mocked. "A blind hog *does* find an acorn every now and then."

Pudgie went next and hit a ball that looked as good as Pecos's when hit, but took a sideways bounce off a rock and rolled against the fence behind the stands.

"Wuzzle frickle snickle!" Pudgie squealed as we laughed. When Pudgie became angry and tried to curse away his frustration it always came out as gibberish.

"Let a man show you how it's done." Pig picked out a ball. His shot landed a few yards from Pecos's ball.

"Good shot!" I complimented him.

"Lucky turd," Pecos pouted.

"Wuzzle fuckle smichicle!" Pudgie mumbled.

I took a ball from the pile and dropped it. I tried to concentrate as I took my stance over the ball, thinking swing slow, keep your head down, all the things you are supposed to do—but rose up at the last instant and topped the ball. The ball took off rolling and bouncing crazily over the rocky ground, and rolled to a stop within yards of the balls of Pig and Pecos, an incredibly lucky result from a bad shot.

"Give me a dad gum break!" Pecos whined in exasperation.

"Frickle pickle brickle!" Pudgie agreed.

"Well planned and well executed," Pig giggled.

"I was aiming a little to the left," I said. "The wind must have gotten it." And giggling, we stalked off after the balls.

Pudgie approached his ball. The ball had rolled to a stop against the chain link fence surrounding the football complex. He would have to take a stance facing the fence and hit the ball left handed to advance it toward the grandstands, or drop fifty paces away and take a five shot penalty. Taking an awkward stance, he turned his club upside down to swing the face of the club toward the ball. He drew back the club and took a jerky swing at the ball. He missed it completely.

"Wuzzle snackle frackle!" He took the stance and swung again. He missed again.

"Mxfle! Flikbp!"

Finally, on his third try, he actually hit the ball and it rolled weakly toward the grandstands.

"Hey! That ain't bad," soothed Pecos. "Your only other option was to go back fifty steps and take a five-shot penalty. You're a whole hell of a lot better off now laying four here than laying six somewhere back there."

"That's true," said Pudgie, calming down somewhat. As he walked to the ball, he dragged his club against the rocky ground.

"What are you doing?" I asked.

"I'm punishing this flingflimmin' club," he said. "I want it to know there's a penalty for doing that. If I scrape some metal off on these rocks, it'll know better than to ever do that again."

"You ought to see the clubs in his bag," Pig laughed. "Every time he hits a bad shot he drags the club along the cart path to the next shot to punish it. He's drug some of them plumb flat on the bottom. He got so mad at a putter that he tried to drag it to death—tied it on the back of his truck with a piece of wire and drug it around behind him until there wasn't anything left but the grip."

"I was with him once when he was dragging that putter around," Pecos joined in the conversation, "and the Highway Patrol stopped us to see what we were dragging. It turned out that the patrolman was a golfer. When Pudgie told him the putter had missed several three-feet putts and cost him a case of beer, the patrolman offered to shoot it for him with his pistol. Pudgie said that'd be too quick, that he wanted it to die a slow painful death draggin' behind his truck. The patrolman just said, 'Go ahead. I won't bother you no more.'"

"I believe in practicin' tough love with my clubs," Pudgie said, taking his normal right-handed stance. "If they know there's a penalty for bad shots they're less likely to transgress. The punished club will talk to the others when he gets back to the bag."

The rest of the round was filled with insulting comments and threats. I got back to the chair designated as home base in twenty-six strokes. Pudgie finished in twenty-four. Pig was the low scorer with seventeen strokes. However, Pecos finished in eighteen. Pig and I lost by one stroke. Pecos and Pudgie whooped and gave each other high fives as Pig and I pouted.

It was late in the day. The sun had begun to dip behind the Twin Peaks. The four of us sat in lawn chairs watching the sunset as we drank the rest of the beer. It was some consolation that Pecos had bought the beer, and Pig and I drank most of it.

"Damn, this is nice!" I said, studying the huge pink and purple cloud formations created by the setting sun. "I can't remember when I've had so much fun playing golf. I sort of feel guilty though. I came here for a relative's funeral, and I wind up having fun with you reprobates."

"Son would have approved," said Pig. "He played with us a couple of times."

"I didn't know you guys knew Son," I said, "or that he played golf."

"I'll remind you again," said Pecos, "Alpine is a small town. Everyone knows everyone—and who the heck ever told you this was golf?"

"Good point."

"What have you got planned for tonight, Toes?" Pecos asked.

"Nothing I'm aware of," I answered as I leaned back and watched the last coloration in the clouds while the day died away entirely.

"Why don't you come go coyote calling with me and Pudgie?"

"Coyote calling!" I mused. "Now there's something I haven't thought of in a long time."

Coyote calling in West Texas meant going out into the country at night with a scoped rifle and a spotlight, and trying to attract coyotes so that they could be shot. The attraction was accomplished by blowing on an instrument, or call, that sounded like an injured rabbit's cries. This sound was irresistible to any hungry coyote within hearing range. The coyote would come running to what it thought were cries from an easy meal. While one hunter was calling, another would sweep the spotlight around, aiming the light just above ground level. The eyes of an approaching coyote glowed like burning coals in the reflected light. As long as the light was not aimed directly into the coyote's eyes, the animal could not detect it. However, the scope on the hunting rifle gathered the light and allowed the hunter to see the approaching coyote well enough to take aim and shoot the animal. Some hunters became so good at making the lure sound like a dying rabbit that they often called the coyote right up to their vehicle and shot the predator at close range with a shotgun.

Ranchers in the area had always looked favorably on coyote calling. Coyotes were a risk to lambs, barn cats, dogs, and even small or injured calves. They were a nuisance, and most ranchers were glad to allow hunters to call and kill the predators on their property. Many ranchers actually paid a bounty on dead coyotes.

"I'd really love to do that," I said, "but I didn't bring any clothes I could wear."

"Shoot, don't worry about that," said Pudgie. "We've got enough stuff here in the field house to suit you out nice and warm. That's no problem."

"What about you, Pig?" Pecos asked. "Want to go out with the real men tonight and remember what it was like before you became a weenie administrator?"

"Actually, I'd love to," answered Pig, "but I have a parent-teacher meeting. Some of us actually work for the money we get from the school district."

"What's that got to do with you?" said Pudgie. "I thought you were an administrator."

Two hours later, after combing through coaching clothes and shoes in the field house and finding suitable garb, I was sitting in the middle seat of Pecos's truck as we drove north out of town. I wore gray coaching pants, a gray, long-sleeved Alpine Bucks sweatshirt, a pair of Pudgie's coaching shoes that were only a little too large, and a purple cap with a big gold A on the front. I also had a sideline jacket for when we actually got out of the truck and hunted. It was warm inside the truck though, and the radio blasted country and western songs at us. This truck was Pecos's pride and joy. It was originally a 1970-something that had been repaired so many times that its age was now indecipherable. Pecos loved the old truck though and took tender care of it.

"Watch out for the gate," Pecos told Pudgie as he squinted into the darkness. "We ought to be there just about now."

"There it is," Pudgie said, as if on cue.

Pecos pulled off the pavement onto a dirt road. A metal gate blocked the way into the pasture beyond. Pudgie got out, unlocked the gate, and walked through while pushing the swinging gate in front of him. Pecos drove the truck through the open gate and a short distance into the pasture. We waited while Pudgie relocked the gate and rejoined us in the cab of the truck, and then followed the dirt road into the darkness beyond. The headlights occasionally revealed brief glimpses of rocky outcrops of hills and mountains. The road was generally flat, though well rutted from frequent travel.

After about thirty minutes, we turned off the road and bumped a short distance across open pasture before Pecos stopped. He turned off the engine and the headlights. We sat quietly for a moment, waiting for the noise to dissipate and for our eyes to adjust to the darkness. Gradually I was able to see that we were parked in a wide, flat valley between low mountains a short distance to either side. In front of the truck I could see nothing but open prairie, an occasional yucca plant dotting the flat grassland. This was a great place to call—we could see a good distance in any direction, and there was little cover to obscure the view of an approaching coyote.

Pecos and Pudgie opened their doors and eased quietly out. I followed. We did not talk. Any sound would carry a great distance on this flat, open ground. We didn't want to spook any prey before even getting started. Pudgie reached behind the seat and pulled a rifle out of the truck. He then reached in again for ammunition. The rifle was a bolt action .30-06 with a scope. Pudgie pushed four shells into the magazine, closed the bolt, and very carefully slipped the safety into place. He made sure I saw where the safety was located and how it operated. I nodded to Pudgie, indicating that I had seen him set the safety and knew how to operate it. He handed me the rifle and reached into the truck again, coming out with a twelve gauge, double-barreled shotgun.

Pecos took a hand-held spotlight from behind the seat on his side. He passed the plug-in back through the open window and plugged it into the cigarette lighter. He then carefully and silently laid the light on top of the cab of the truck. Pudgie had already climbed over the side into the bed of the truck. Pecos climbed up with him. When they were both in, I carefully handed the two weapons up to Pudgie and climbed in myself. Pecos turned the spotlight on for a test. He swept it in a circle around us. The light lit up the terrain brightly for a distance of about fifty yards, less brightly for another hundred or so, and them very dimly for an indiscernible distance beyond that. Satisfied, Pecos turned off the light and took the wooden caller from his shirt pocket. He placed the instrument to his lips and blew. A piercing, high-pitched, squeaking sound came from the call, and as Pecos blew less and less air the sound trailed off, softer and softer until it was gone. After each call he waited a few moments and repeated the process. To hungry coyotes, the squeaking sounded enough like a dying rabbit to bring them running.

Every several minutes Pecos stopped calling, turned on the spotlight and aimed it just above the ground. After a complete turn, when we saw nothing, he took up the call and began blowing into it again.

For half an hour we saw nothing as Pecos searched with the light, but then, slightly off to the right of the front of the truck, we saw two small reflections of light bobbing beneath the spotlight beam. The light was reflecting off the eyes of a rapidly approaching coyote. Pecos and Pudgie both nudged me.

"I see it," I whispered. I looked through the scope of the .30-06, and could clearly see the coyote loping toward us. I flipped off the safety with my right thumb as I waited for the coyote to stop or slow so that I'd have a good shot. Pecos resumed calling while Pudgie took the spotlight and tried to keep it steady just above the coyote.

Abruptly, the coyote stopped running to listen and smell. He stood tall, his ears standing straight up as he focused on the sound of the call. I steadied the crosshairs inside the scope directly between the two glowing eyes, and gently pulled the trigger. Boom! The shot exploded in my ears and the rifle kicked back hard against my shoulder. I instantly lost sight of the coyote in the scope as the gun jumped upward. Pudgie lowered the light full on the animal as soon as I fired and the ground was illuminated brightly for the fifty yards to the coyote, who was still rolling backwards from the high caliber bullet's impact. For an instant he violently kicked his legs, raising a cloud of dust from the dry ground, and then lay totally still, as the dust slowly settled.

"No baby rabbit for you tonight!" Pudgie said with a satisfied snort.

"Good shot, Toes!" exclaimed Pecos. "Living in the big city hasn't hurt your shooting any."

"I still shoot a little," I explained, looking at the dead coyote, which looked small and scruffy in death. "I take my son target shooting in Austin."

"Crap, now we'll have to hit our shots or be embarrassed by a city boy," Pudgie said.

"All right, Pudgie, you're up," Pecos said as he began blowing on the call again. We would deal with the dead coyote later. Even though the report of the rifle would have scared most animals away, the call was an irresistible lure for hungry predators. It was not uncommon for a coyote fleeing the sound of a gunshot to hear the calls, turn around, and come right back to the sound and the waiting gun. I passed the scoped rifle to Pudgie and took the shotgun in return. I laid the shotgun on the top of the cab and took up the spotlight. Pudgie operated the bolt action of the rifle to inject another round into the firing chamber.

After half an hour, during which we had seen no other coyotes, Pudgie said, "Hold on awhile, Pecos. I've got to pee."

He handed me the rifle and climbed over the side of the truck's bed to the ground.

"Hand me the shotgun, will you, Toes? I might have to blast a rattlesnake. A lonesome snake might think he's seen a relative when I pull my Pecos out and come to visit."

I chuckled as I handed it down to him. "Shine the light down here to make sure I'm not on top of a snake now, will you, Pecos?" Pecos shined the spotlight around Pudgie's feet. Seeing no snakes, he turned off the light, and we listened to the splashing sound Pudgie made as he played, drawing circles on the ground and such, as he urinated.

"Hey, Pecos," Pudgie said in a soft voice that got our attention. "Shine the light in the front of the trunk. I think I see something there."

Pecos directed the spotlight directly over the hood of the truck to the ground in front. It took us a second or two to realize what we saw. A full-grown mountain lion was sitting on the ground a few feet from the truck. A dirty brown color, he sat on his rear haunches with his front legs straight supporting his upper body. His tail was lying on the ground behind him, the last few inches curled upward and moving from side to side. He was peering up at Pecos and me, not expecting to find us at the end of his stalk, and seemed to be taking a timeout to explore his options.

"Holy crap!" said Pecos, and in his excitement the light jiggled about around the mountain cat.

"Son of a gun!" I jerked the rifle up into position to fire.

"Muxle! Fluxle!" Pudgie squealed as he tried to get the shotgun into firing position.

I quickly pointed the rifle in the general direction of the big cat, which was springing into a run, and pulled the trigger. Pudgie jerked the shotgun toward the cat and pulled both barrels at once.

Boom! I squeezed off a shot. The shotgun discharging both barrels at once made twice as big a boom. The sounds of the guns firing were followed immediately with metallic sounds. The three of us were frozen in place, but the big cat was long gone. We hadn't come near hitting him. Then we became aware of a hissing sound.

"You shot my truck!" Pecos screamed. I recognized the hissing sound then. One of us had hit a tire.

"Of all the damned idiots!" said Pecos as he jumped to the ground. He directed the spotlight onto the front of the truck.

My shot had entered the top of the hood and exited the front just below the crest. Two perfectly round holes showed the bullet's path. Pudgie's shotgun blast had sent hundreds of lead pellets into the right front fender and tire. The tire was flat, and the fender was covered with small indentations and holes where the pellets had hit.

Pecos continued to rant as he paced in front of his truck examining the damage. "You goddamned idiots shot my truck!" he shouted in disbelief.

"Well shoot, Pecos," said Pudgie defensively, "that was a damn big mountain lion. He could've drug me off in the weeds and eaten me while you guys picked your noses in the truck."

"That *was* a big cat!" I chimed in, in embarrassed agreement, following Pecos as he surveyed destruction we had wrought on his prized possession. "Scared the poop out of me. We had to shoot quick or lose our chance."

"Damn!" Pudgie gave a little shiver. "I've never been that close to one outside a zoo. That spooked me!"

"I can see that," Pecos said suddenly, starting to laugh. He shone the spotlight on Pudgie. I looked at Pudgie and also began to laugh.

"What do you mean?" Pudgie asked, looking puzzled.

"Look at your pants," I said as Pecos and I laughed harder.

Pudgie looked down, "Gloflx dugkem!" he shouted.

His gray coaching pants were dark with a wet stain from his crotch to his shoes…on both legs. "Dammit! I was peein' already when that cat looked at me—lickin' his chops like I was dinner. I just forgot to stop peein' before I shot. He didn't make me do this!"

Pecos and I were laughing too hard to respond.

"Muckzle fluczle glyzzx!" Pudgie cursed, looking helplessly at his pants. He knew that this would stay with him forever. It was too great to fade away. "Come on guys," he pleaded. "You both know I was already peeing when we saw that monster. You'd have peed all over yourself too. Did you think I'd stick my Johnson back in my pants and zip up before firing? He would've been gone by then."

"Except you didn't shoot the cat!" Pecos laughed. "You *murdered* my truck! Did you think it was going to attack you too?"

"The good news," I said, "is that you didn't try to pee on it while you stuck the shotgun in your pants and blew your gonads off." Pecos and I squealed in laughter. Pecos leaned on the front of the truck for support, and I tried to catch my breath from the effort expended in the laughing, my sides aching.

Finally Pudgie began to smile, and then laugh at the absurd episode. "Just one thing, Pecos. Can I mount this fender over my fireplace?" he asked. "I've never killed a truck before."

After several minutes of laughing, we finally got around to inspecting the truck more closely to determine if there was irreparable damage. My shot had passed cleanly through the front of the hood without hitting anything inside, so there was no damage to the engine. Pudgie's blast had clearly killed the right front tire, but the pellets hadn't penetrated into anything beyond the tire. The fender was peppered with buckshot indentations, but there was no damage to anything except the tire.

"Nothing here a good body shop can't fix in a day," I said. "And we'll get you a new tire when we get back to town."

"Oh no!" Pecos replied, an amused grin spreading his cheeks, "I ain't gettin' this fixed. I'm going to drive it like this from now on to remind everyone of the idiots I'm cursed to hang out with!"

Pudgie and I begged Pecos to get the truck fixed, volunteering to pay for the repairs and even a new paint job for the whole vehicle. But Pecos quickly saw the story value of the truck's damage, and wasn't about to cover it up. Pudgie and I had accidentally gifted him with a great show-and-tell story for as long as he had this truck, which he had already intended to keep for the rest of his life. Pudgie and I were done for. We intuitively knew that our only chance to salvage any dignity was to embellish the story ourselves.

I immediately began thinking of ways to make our part in this debacle seem heroic rather than something out of a Three Stooges movie. The only acceptable defense in a situation like this was an aggressive offense.

"All right," Pudgie said. "I confess. This was my stab at a mercy killing. You aren't never gonna let this old truck die a dignified death, so I tried to put it out of its misery. I can't help it if I have a soft heart."

"I don't know about that," I said. "But if you hadn't panicked and almost knocked me out of the truck, Pecos, I would've hit him right between the eyes. It's hard to be accurate when the guy holding the light is trampling you trying to get away."

"Bull!" Pecos said with a snort. "Neither of those phony stories will hold any air."

"Then we'll just have to think of better ones," I laughed, with a wink at Pudgie. "In the meantime, shouldn't we change this tire?"

Pecos replied, "I'm not squatting down on top of a rattlesnake. Let's wait till morning when we can see what we're doing."

"Good idea," Pudgie said as he cautiously looked around. "I've already spent more time tromping around out here in the dark than I care to."

"What are we going to do?" I asked. "Sleep in the truck?"

"Yep. It won't be so bad," Pecos said as he opened the driver's side door. He reached behind the seat to pull out two small cardboard boxes. "Here's an air mattress that fits the truck bed, and a pump that runs off the battery."

He plugged the pump into the cigarette lighter socket after he removed the spotlight. "Hold this," he said, as he handed me a flashlight. He pulled a folded air mattress out of the other box. I illuminated the work for him as he attached the other connection on the pump to the mattress and switched on the pump. The pump emitted an annoying whine, but quickly inflated the mattress. When it was fully inflated, Pecos flipped the mattress over the side into the bed of the truck.

"Darn. That's pretty neat," I said.

"Yeah, a queen-sized air mattress just fits the bed of this model truck," Pecos said. He replaced the pump apparatus behind the seat and pulled out a plastic bag that had something soft in it. "This is a sleeping bag," said Pecos. "But it unfolds into a very nice quilt that just covers the bed. Perfect fit all the way around."

"Mind if I ask why you have a mattress and bedding in your truck?"

"Two reasons," Pecos replied. "First, if the wife and I are driving around and get excited, we can pull off almost anywhere. Second, when Pudgie's wife kicks him out of the house he comes over to my house, and this gives him a place to sleep that's outside. He doesn't disturb anything me and the old lady are engaged in inside."

"One time!" Pudgie lamented as he unloaded the two rifles and placed them back behind the seat. "One time I got kicked out for a night, and he makes it sound like he has to have the truck bed ready every dadgummed night!"

"Just exactly how are we going to do this?" I asked.

"We'll sleep in the truck bed, on the mattress, under the sleeping bag," said Pecos

"No, I mean who has to sleep next to Pudgie. He has pee all over him. He smells like a bus station urinal."

"Well we could make him take off his pants," Pecos laughed, "but I don't want to be under the covers with him with his thing loose. You never can tell what kind of latent tendencies are lurking in what passes for a mind in his head."

"Eeeeewwwww!" I said in disgust. "I'm sleeping in the cab."

"Oh, okay," Pecos laughed. "I'll sleep next to him. We're all going to smell like pee when we get home anyway." And, laughing good-naturedly, we climbed into the bed of the truck. When we had settled in and spread the opened sleeping bag over the three of us, I was surprised at how comfortable it was. I used a rolled up sweatshirt as a pillow, lying on my back. Looking up I was once more surprised by how many stars were visible out here in the middle of nowhere.

"I had forgotten there were so many stars in the sky," I said. "With all the ground light in Austin I'd guess we can see about ten percent of what I see right now."

"It's really something isn't it?" Pecos answered. "I never get tired of sleeping out and just looking at them. Look at the Milky Way. It's really pretty tonight."

"It's part of the bonus we get for living out here," said Pudgie.

I asked, "Do you guys ever feel like you're missing something living in a small town so far away from everything? Do you ever wish you'd gone somewhere bigger?"

"Like what?" Pecos asked. "You just said you never see a night sky like this where you live, and when's the last time you went hunting, or even played golf like we did today?"

"When's the last time a mountain lion snuck up and sniffed your butt?" said Pudgie. "And how many adventures are you going to have like the one we had tonight? What could we be missing?"

"Well, the symphony, nice restaurants, and shopping malls," I answered a little defensively.

"You go to the symphony a lot, do you, Toes?" Pudgie had an amused tone.

"Once or twice a year I guess." I thought how lame that sounded and quickly added, "But I know I could always go if I wanted to."

"Your restaurants serve Mexican food any better than the Casa?" said Pecos.

"Not any better, but there's more of them," I protested.

"Can you eat in more than one at a time?" Pudgie asked, now thoroughly enjoying the conversation.

Pudgie said, "I go to a restaurant to eat, and if the one I like has the best food, I don't see any use in going to another one. On top of that, since most of Alpine goes there, I know everyone. It's like a family meal. Gives me a chance to catch up on all the news."

"There's a lot to be said for familiarity and consistency," said Pecos. "It makes all of us closer because we see one another all the time. In a way, we are a big family and I like that. Most of the time anyway. When's the last time you had as much fun as you've had today?"

"You got me there," I said. "I can't even remember any time I had this much fun."

"On the other hand," I said after a moment of silence, "when I go to the symphony no one pees all over themselves, and even if they did I sure as hell wouldn't have to sleep with them afterward."

"Ahh, you only notice it for the first two or three hours," Pecos chuckled. "And besides, that smell will keep any varmints from jumping in here with us."

"That's right!" Pudgie snorted, pulling the cover to his chin. "You should thank me for protecting you instead of hurting my feelings."

"I'm sorry, Pudgie," I said. "I plumb forgot how sensitive you are."

We talked and laughed and reminisced for hours. When the conversation died down, Pudgie and Pecos started snoring, almost in harmony. I lay there in the truck bed, admiring the stars, and listened to my two old friends snore.

"When was the last time I'd had this much fun?" I couldn't think of a single time.

Chapter 19

The sun coming up over the mountains to the east roused us from the pickup bed. After changing the flat tire and driving into Alpine, Pecos, Pudgie, and I ate breakfast at a truck stop on the edge of town. We then went back to the football field house where I showered and changed for the funeral service.

I had agreed to meet Billy Rex at the church. He and I both arrived at the First Baptist Church a few minutes before one o'clock and parked across the street in the Thriftway Supermarket lot, as the church lot was already mostly full. As we walked across the street to the church, I inspected the building I had entered many times as a child going to Sunday school and church. The church was an imposing, dark brick structure with a curious domed roof over the center. I suddenly realized that I had seen this building before—it was almost an exact copy of Monticello, Thomas Jefferson's home in Virginia. The entrance to the church was a large covered porch flanked by huge white columns, and covered by the peaked false front—classical Greek architecture Jefferson was said to have copied.

As we walked up the steps I had a flash memory of a Sunday school class with kids in a row singing, "Jesus loves you, this I know, cause the Bible tells you so."

Inside, the church had changed a little in forty years—some new paint and new cushions on the pews—but it was still mostly as I remembered it. Dark oak pews formed a semicircle around the altar, which was in a corner of the large sanctuary. There was a balcony, also a semicircle, which covered about half of the lower level. The pews were covered with burgundy cushions, and the floor was carpeted in the same color. The minister's lectern stood at the front of the altar stage, with four rows of choir seats behind. Above the choir seats, recessed into the wall, was the baptismal tank always found in Baptist churches. I was surprised that I was still a little intimidated by the place, more than forty years after having had the devil scared out of me by fire-breathing Baptist ministers.

Billy Rex and I found seats in the first few rows, designated for "FAMILY MEMBERS" by signs placed at the end of each of the rows. The first-floor seats were almost filled, and the balcony was more than half full. The eclectic crowd wore everything from jeans and boots to business suits. A full third of the men held cowboy hats on their laps.

I recognized almost everyone in the family section. Charlie was sitting on the first row with Roy Don and his wife. Next to them were Starlene and her husband Vernon. Crystal and her husband also sat on the front row but were separated from the other siblings by individuals I did not recognize. Billy Rex and I sat on the outside end of the second row with Robert Earl and his sister Blossom on the opposite end of the row. Aunt Frances sat in the middle of the row with Ida and Vera, her half sisters from Grandfather's second marriage. Roughly a dozen other relatives filled the remaining reserved seats. I managed to catch a few eyes, nodded in greeting and silently mouthed hellos.

Son's coffin had been placed on the floor level in front of the altar. The top had once more been removed to reveal Son. Above him, seated near the lectern was the minister, dressed in a dark suit. However, there was not a choir. Sitting on the front row of the choir pews were what appeared to be six working cowboys, all in pressed jeans and white shirts buttoned to the top. Boots were the standard footgear, and cowboy hats rested on the pew beside them. There were also several guitars, a fiddle, and a base fiddle—a western band, I thought.

I had little time to wonder about the choir. At a nod from the minister, the six men stood and took up their instruments but did not start playing. One stepped forward and hushed the crowd as he sang, without any music, in a clear baritone voice. He immediately captured everyone's undivided attention as he began singing the sad old cowboy lament, "Streets of Laredo."

"As I walked out in the streets of Laredo,
As I walked out in Laredo one day,
I spied a poor cowboy all wrapped in white linen,
Wrapped in white linen as cold as the clay."

His clear, sad voice penetrated every corner of the old church. As he reached the chorus the other cowboys began to play their instruments as they sang with him.

"Oh beat the drum slowly and play the fife lowly,
Play the dead march as you carry me along;
Take me to the green valley, there lay the sod o'er me,
For I'm a young cowboy, and I know I'm goin' home."

Then the soloist continued alone with the next verse, his mournful voice the only sound in the church.

"Get six jolly cowboys to carry my coffin;
Get six pretty maidens to sing me a song;
Put bunches of roses all over my coffin,
Put roses to deaden the sods as they fall."

This time the soloist signaled for the audience to join in and sing the chorus with them.

"Oh, beat the drum slowly and play the fife lowly,
Play the dead march as they carry me along;
Take me to the green valley, there lay the sod o'er me,
For I'm a young cowboy and I know I'm goin' home."

And the single cowboy soloist sang,

"Then swing your rope slowly and rattle your spurs lowly,
And give a wild whoop as you carry me along;
And in the grave throw me and roll the sod o'er me,
For I'm a young cowboy and I know I'm goin' home."

And all of us sang loudly on the chorus, now fully captured by the song and the moment,

"Oh beat the drum slowly and play the fife lowly,
Play the dead march as you carry me along;
Take me to the green valley, there lay the sod o'er me,
For I'm a young cowboy and I know I'm goin' home."

And the lone cowboy continued,

"Go bring me a cup, a cup of cold water,
To cool my parched lips, the cowboy then said;
Before I returned his soul had departed,
And gone to the round-up, the cowboy was gone."

Everyone sang again,

"Oh beat the drum slowly and play the fife lowly,
Play the dead march as you carry me along;
Take me to the green valley, there lay the sod o'er me,
For I'm a young cowboy and I know I'm goin' home."

The band sat down, and the soloist finished the song, gradually slowing the tempo as he reached the end of the song,

"We beat the drum slowly and played the fife lowly,
And we bitterly wept as we bore him along;
For we all loved our comrade, so brave, young, and handsome,
We all loved the cowboy who had gone on alone."

The cowboy soloist let his voice trail away, dropped his head, and turned to sit with his mates. Many in the audience were weeping openly, and even the hardest looking cowboys were wiping their eyes with handkerchiefs. As I reached for my own handkerchief, I heard Billy Rex sniffing loudly beside me.

For a few moments the church was quiet save for sniffing and nose blowing. We savored a wonderfully tender moment. Then, slowly, the minister arose from his seat and approached the lectern. He was a portly man, average height, a receding hairline—an appearance soft enough to indicate his profession in just about any crowd. He wiped at his eyes with a handkerchief as he walked forward. He paused a moment, cleared his throat, and began to speak.

"We are gathered here today to honor and say farewell to John Wesley Cable, cowboy, better known by his nickname, Son. Son attended this church his entire life, and it was my pleasure to be his minister for the last eight years. Son knew for several years now that he had a heart condition that would likely take his life if he continued as a cowboy—but Son wanted to end his life as he had lived it. Knowing that time might be short, Son wrote his own eulogy and gave it to me a few months ago, asking that I read it at his funeral if the worst happened. I read to you now in Son Cable's own words."

And then Son spoke to us, through the minister, "If you are hearing this it means the doctors were right and I am gone." There was a pause. "I hate it that I actually proved the doctors right after all the times I tried to prove them wrong. Oh well, the law of averages had to catch up with them sooner or later."

A small chuckle murmured through the congregation.

"If we really believe what we all claim to believe though, don't feel bad for me. I've gone on to a better place. I'm probably riding the prairie with my father right now. We're having a great time, and I'll save a spot at the bunkhouse table for each of you, though not too soon, I hope."

The audience nodded and smiled and even chuckled, most remembering the man, but I remembered the boy.

"I've had a wonderful life, and I wouldn't change a single moment of it. From my earliest memory I knew what I wanted to do, be a cowboy. That's all I ever wanted. And I was blessed. I realized my dream and lived it every day. How many people can say that?

"So please do not see this as a sad occasion, but as a happy time. Be happy for me that I lived a full life, and now get to continue it with my father and many other old cowboys who have gone on before. However, I do ask you to indulge me one sad song. My favorite song since childhood was a cowboy song my father and uncles taught me. I'd like 'Little Joe the Wrangler' to be sung at my funeral.

"I've asked my friends to have a party the evening of my funeral to celebrate my life. I hope all my friends and family will participate. It's been a great ride, but it's time to put the horses in the barn and call it a day. God bless all of you."

When the minister folded the paper from which he had been reading, almost as a single person the crowd let out a collective sigh. I hadn't realized that I'd been holding my breath as I focused on the Son Cable's last words. There were audible sobs and much blowing of noses into handkerchiefs.

"Tonight," the minister said, "I've been told there will be a cowboy wake at Casa Blanca, in accordance with Son's wishes. It starts at seven, and everyone is invited. Now we'll hear some more special music."

The six-man cowboy band rose and began to play and sing the old cowboy song I'd heard my father sing hundreds of times, "Little Joe the Wrangler."

"Oh, Little Joe the Wrangler will wrangle nevermore;
His days with the remuda they are o'er.
'Twas a year ago last April that he rode into our camp,
Just a little Texas stray and all alone.

It was late in the evening when he rode into our camp
On a little Texas pony he called Chaw.
With his brogan shoes and overalls, a tougher lookin' kid
You never in your life before had saw.

His saddle was a Texas kack built many years ago.
An OK spur on one foot lightly swung.
With his pack roll in a cotton sack loosely tied behind
And a canteen from his saddle horn was hung.

He said he'd had to leave his home, his ma had married twice;
His new pa whipped him every day or two.
So he saddled up old Chaw one night and quietly rode away
And now he's trying to paddle his own canoe.

He said if we would give him work he'd do the best he could
Although he did know nothing about a cow.
So the boss he cut him out a mount and kindly helped him on
'Cause he sorta liked that Texas stray somehow.

He learned to wrangle horses and learned to know them all,
And to get them in at daybreak if he could.
And to trail the old chuck wagon and always hitch the team,
And to help the cook each evening rustle wood.

We herded up the Pecos, the weather bein' fine,
We camped down by the south side of the bend.
When a norther started blowin', we called the extra guard
'Cause it took us all to hold the cattle in.

Now, Little Joe the Wrangler was called out with the rest,
The lad had scarcely gotten to that herd,
When those cattle they stampeded like a hail storm on they fled,
And all of us was ridin' for the head.

Midst the flashes of the lightnin' a horseman we could see:
It was Little Joe the Wrangler in the lead.

He was ridin' Old Blue Rocket with his slicker o'er his head;
He was trying to turn those cattle in the lead.

At last we got them millin' and kinda settled down,
When the extra guards back to the wagon went.
But there was one a-missin', we saw it at a glance;
'Twas our little Texas stray, poor Wrangler Joe.

Next mornin' just at daybreak, we found where Rocket fell
Down in a washout twenty feet below.
Beneath his horse's body, his spur had rung his knell,
Was our little Texas stray, poor Wrangler Joe."

Everyone listened attentively to the mournful ballad that had been sung around cowboy campfires for over a hundred years. Most in the church were Texans who had lived in or were raised in ranching country. We had all heard the song. The words sometimes changed a little, depending on who was singing, but the story was always the same. The poor kid from a broken home, who ran away to avoid abuse, was taken in by kindly cowboys, and died trying to help his benefactors stop a stampede, a cowboy's worst nightmare. I remembered my father and Son's father playing while Uncle Ray joined in the singing around campfires in Fort Davis. The line where the boy's single spur had rung his death knell always broke my heart. I believe that the story of the boy's short and sad life set most of us to thinking about our own lives—and we were grateful. I think that was Son's gift to us.

After the song ended, the minister said, "As Son wished, we will complete the service at graveside." The ushers began directing the people from the pews, in an orderly continuous line, to file by and view the body for one last time, and then move out the door of the church. It was a slow process, and the family remained seated until the last. Pecos and Pudgie, with their wives, were among the mourners. Each mourner, after viewing the body, walked past the family section. Many paused to speak, usually offering condolences and hugs. As Pecos was shaking hands with Vernon and Starlene, his wife leaned over to me, "Couldn't you have done enough damage to that old truck to kill it? A great shot you are," she said with a twinkle in her eyes. Pudgie's wife just looked at me and rolled her eyes.

Finally the family members walked by the open coffin. I paused for a moment to take one last look at my cousin. "Damn fine exit, cowboy," I muttered under my breath. "Damned fine exit."

Emerging from the church, I was surprised to see an unpainted, uncovered buckboard wagon hitched to a six-horse team in the street near the door. Two cowboys held six more horses, all saddled, behind the wagon.

After everyone was out of the church, the six cowboys from the band carried the now closed casket out, down the steps, and placed it in the back of the wagon. The two cowboys holding the saddled horses passed the reins to the band members-turned-pallbearers, who mounted as the first two climbed onto the seat of the wagon. With a snap of the reins by one of the wagon drivers, the horse-drawn funeral wagon rolled away from the church. The six mounted pallbearers fell in behind the wagon, riding two abreast.

Several men began directing cars and trucks into a column behind the wagon and horsemen for the short drive to the cemetery. Billy Rex rode with me in my truck as we pulled into a place near the front of the line.

City policemen were stopping and directing traffic. The wagon and horsemen, followed by what seemed like a hundred or more vehicles—more pickup trucks than automobiles—rolled slowly over to Holland Street, and then left onto it for about six blocks. Turning right onto Highway 118, the slow-moving procession rolled past the Sul Ross University football stadium and the Casa Blanca Bar and Grill, heading toward the cemetery. A short distance down Highway 118 the procession turned left through a residential neighborhood to the cemetery on the edge of town. It had been a journey of less than a mile, but took more than half an hour to complete following the slow moving wagon.

Citizens of Alpine who were stopped at intersections by the funeral procession at first reacted to the unusual conveyance with expressions signaling astonishment, then, realizing what was happening, most smiled in approval and waited patiently. Some got out of their vehicles and stood in silent respect while the wagon passed. People on Holland Street stood in quiet attention, removing their hats, as the wagon moved by. It was the most dignified funeral procession I'd ever been part of.

When the caravan arrived at the cemetery, the wagon inched its way to the prepared gravesite near the front of the cemetery. The cowboy pallbearers dismounted and handed the reins to the two wagon drivers. They waited as the rest of us entered the cemetery and parked. Everyone exited their vehicles and walked to the gravesite.

A canvas awning had been erected next to the open grave. Underneath the awning were about twenty folding chairs for the family. Billy Rex and I took seats to the back of the area. Other attendees gathered and stood around the awning and gravesite.

Son had picked a great day to be buried, I thought. It was a beautiful crisp, clear fall day. A Mountain and SR Mountain stood out starkly as I looked from the awning, across the open grave. Behind us stretched a wide grassy valley reaching off toward blue mountains in the distance. Red and white cattle could be seen grazing in the valley.

When everyone was settled, the six cowboys removed the coffin from the wagon and sat it on the apparatus over the grave. They took off their hats and stood in a line on the opposite side of the coffin from the awning. When they removed their hats, so did everyone else.

Then a single cowboy walked from the crowd and stood at the head of the coffin, holding his large white cowboy hat over his breast.

"My name is Red Odell," he said, "and Son was a friend of mine. I don't know how many of you know that Son loved cowboy poetry. He asked that one of his favorites be read today." Red Odell was a tall, lean man who looked like he'd worked hard every day of his life. He did indeed have red hair and a big red handlebar mustache. He wore jeans, boots, and a white shirt buttoned to the top. He reached into his breast pocket and pulled out a sheet of paper, which he held with his right hand, holding his hat by his side in his left.

"The poem I'm going to read was written by a Nevada cowboy named Jack Walther. It's called 'Ruby Mountains.'"

> "I am part of this range of waving grass,
> Part of the evening breeze, the gentle rains that pass.
> I am the horse or range cow that moves out there so free.
> Deep down within, they seem a part of me.
>
> I am the snows on the mountain that cause the streams to flow,
> Spreading out on the valley, urging the grass to grow.
> The meadow in the valley, the leaves and branches of a tree,
> They are more than a thing of beauty. They are a part of me.
>
> I am the buttercups blooming in the springtime,
> The call of the blue grouse on the hill,
> The piece and quiet of a summer night
> When all the world is still.

I am the sparkling stars on a winter night,
Or a crisp cold morning sun.
I am the gurgling protesting stream,
Beneath the winter ice shall run.

The coyote that howls in the evening or the hoot owl in the wood,
I sense them stir within my soul. Deep down it feels so good.
With all this a part of me, I can never be alone.
I am the richest man on earth, for all this I own.

When this body that you see is stilled,
Stand not by my grave and cry.
When a part of these things,
I will be renewed and shall never die.

But come out in the spring grass,
See the songbirds up in the tree,
Just relax, spend some time,
It is there I shall forever be."

He folded the paper and put it back into his pocket, turned, and walked back into the circle of mourners. Except for soft sobs, there was absolute silence.

The minister walked to the coffin to say a brief prayer, then, "This concludes our service. On behalf of the family, thank you all for coming, and please remember the cowboy wake this evening at seven at Casa Blanca. It's in Son's honor, and you're all invited."

Nothing happened. Everyone sat or stood motionless. None of us wanted it to be over. Finally, slowly, one by one, the cowboys put their hats back on and began to drift back to their vehicles. The crowd began to quietly dissolve. There was transition into hand shaking, hugging, and "I'm so glad you could make it." I found myself standing with Billy Rex a little apart from the remaining, milling mourners.

"Wasn't that just the most impressive thing you have ever seen?" a voice asked, and I turned to see Robert Earl approaching with his hand outstretched. I had seen him in the crowd, but this was the first time either of us had had the chance to speak. Robert Earl was now a slender, almost frail man. His very short hair showed gray speckles. A neatly trimmed mustache punctuated his thin face. He wore a dark gray suit, white shirt, and wine-colored tie.

Taking his outstretched hand, I said, "Unbelievable. I've never seen anything like it."

"I have never been so moved at a funeral," Robert Earl said, incredulously. "I almost wanted to applaud when it was over, and I'm about the furthest thing from a cowboy you'll ever find. Are you going to the wake this evening?"

"Wild horses couldn't keep me away," I assured him.

No one noticed a dirty, white pickup parked alone just outside the cemetery, away from the funeral activity.

Chapter 20

My original plan had been to visit with relatives at the Cable house after the funeral. Good manners in West Texas dictated that, after a funeral, friends and family congregate at the bereaved's home to commiserate, visit, and eat a meal if the timing were appropriate. To not do so would be a breach of etiquette. I had figured I would visit for only long enough to be considered socially acceptable, then leave and drive back to Austin, stopping along the way if I got tired. Staying for the cowboy wake would require a change in plans, which I mentioned to Billy Rex and Robert Earl.

"That's right," replied Robert Earl. "I'd planned to start back right after the funeral too. I hadn't thought about staying tonight."

"Me neither," said Billy Rex. "Where can we stay?" We considered the various motels in Alpine.

As we were talking, Charlie walked over from the tight knot of family members still consoling one another beneath the awning. In his mid-fifties, Charlie was still a strikingly handsome man. His sandy blond hair, stylishly long, was graying at the temples only, and a crisp mustache was still sandy blond. He appeared to have gained no weight in the thirty years since his playing days, and he moved with a grace that announced that he was a serious athlete. He wore an expensive tan tweed sport coat, cream-colored trousers, and tasseled loafers. A white silk shirt and silk Italian tie completed the ensemble. He looked as if he had walked right off a fashion show runway to come to the cemetery.

"Howdy, cousins," he said with what actually might have been a sincere smile, a smile that framed very white and very expertly engineered teeth. "It's good to see all you guys again. It's been way too long." He shook hands all around as we echoed his sentiments. I noticed he practiced a kind of fake sincerity evidenced by grasping each of us on the shoulder with his left hand while he shook with his right and looking seriously into our eyes for just a second before moving on to the next.

Charlie, Billy Rex, Robert Earl, and I stood talking and catching up like people who hadn't seen one another in ages, which was actually the case. After a few moments Robert Earl excused himself to go greet an acquaintance he had noticed in the dwindling crowd, now drifting away.

"Tommy!" A loud, commanding female voice startled me. I turned to see Aunt Ida approaching, aided by her wooden cane. Aunt Ida was my father's half-sister by Grandfather's second marriage. In her early seventies, she looked to still be in remarkably good health. She was thin, taller than the average woman, which caused her to have to stoop a little to get a good brace from her cane. Her fully gray hair was topped with a small round hat that complemented her dress, which was black with a small floral pattern.

She stalked as purposefully as the cane would allow right up to me. I could smell her perfume, which I remembered from childhood. Her cheeks were rouged and she had bright red lips. She may have been old, but her dark brown eyes were bright and alert.

"It's about time you came to see us!" she barked harshly at me, and then softened her tone as she addressed the entire group. "It's so nice to see you boys all together again just like when you were kids. You're coming over to the house to eat now, aren't you." It was not a question, but an affirmation. We understood her command.

"Why of course, Aunt Ida," I said in a hasty, sincere reply. "I'm looking forward to seeing everyone."

Out of the corner of my eye I noticed Robert Earl moving slowly back toward us arm in arm with Aunt Vera, the oldest sister from the first marriage. Vera was eighty, and wobbled unsteadily on Robert Earl's arm. I could hear her shoes rattling on the gravel covering the road as she slid her feet along, never fully losing contact with the ground.

"Where's the little sissy?" Aunt Ida blurted out. "Didn't you boys have him over here earlier?"

I grimaced and she noticed my reaction. Aunt Ida twisted her face into the look of someone who had just tasted something sour.

"He's right behind me, isn't he?" she said, knowing he was, and that she'd just committed what most would consider a social blunder.

"Aunt Ida! How nice to see you," Robert Earl exclaimed with exaggerated friendliness. "And how nice of you to inquire about me."

Ida turned and saw Vera on Robert Earl's arm. "Vera, dammit!" she exclaimed. "I've told you and told you not to sneak up behind me like that!" She grabbed Vera's arm and hustled her toward the cars, without acknowledging Robert Earl or indicating that she might have done something wrong.

"Kiss my ass, Ida!" Aunt Vera replied as the two of them wobbled away. The two sisters had cursed at one another for as long as anyone could remember. It was really an expression of love and their comfort with one another, plus they both loved shocking people. Little old ladies can get away with anything.

"We'll see you boys at the house," Aunt Ida said loudly back over her shoulder as she sped Vera away at the speed of a racing snail.

"Nice to know Vera and Ida haven't changed," Robert Earl said, as he watched them inching toward their waiting ride. He showed no reaction to Ida's remark. Billy Rex and Charlie were intently studying the horizon while pretending they had heard nothing of the exchange.

"I'm sorry about that, Robert Earl," I said.

"Oh hell! Don't let that worry you. I stopped worrying about Aunt Ida's disapproval years ago. I enjoy getting under her skin. I drive her crazy, but deep down I think she enjoys the annoyance. You know she and Vera are two strange old bats. The two things they enjoy most in life are irritating other people and being irritated. Gives their lives spice. She was just as likely to have said the same thing if she'd known I was there."

"Let's go to the house," Billy Rex suggested, and we moved quickly, relieved to walk away from the embarrassment Vera had left in her wake.

The drive to the Cable's old house on the west side of Alpine took only a few minutes. Thirty or forty cars were parked in front of the house and in a vacant lot across the street. We parked my truck in the vacant lot and Billy Rex and I walked through thigh-high weeds to the street, which was still unpaved, and across to the house. When we were kids here this house had been well outside of town proper, and even now was still on the very outer edge of development. There were still vacant lots directly in front of and to the side of the house. Behind the house I could still see open pastures toward the towering Twin Peaks. An occasional house dotted the landscape in that direction, but it was still almost as open as it had been when we were kids. As I looked toward the mountains I saw the shadows of clouds moving rapidly across the landscape like a cat crossing a yard, smooth and supple, caressing and molding to the terrain as it moved over it.

As we came into the yard the scene resembled lunch break on a western movie set. We were surrounded by men in boots, jeans, and western hats. They were sitting in lawn chairs, standing, or squatted down—sitting on their heels in a stance my father had called "hunkering down"—talking, drinking coffee, hanging out, just being there. I saw several relatives and a few faces I recognized. Grandma Myrtle was rocking on the porch; she was Grandfather's youngest sister, now ninety-two. Years ago, the Cables had built a small one-room guest house out back of the main house for visitors and relatives. Myrtle lived there now, maintaining some independence while actually being cared for by family. I made a mental note to visit her before I left.

I moved from group to group, shaking hands, acknowledging the people I knew and introducing myself to those I didn't. I heard snatches of conversations:

"You still workin' for the Highway Department?"

"What's that you're driving now, a Dodge? Had any trouble with it?"

"Yes, I think I remember that. In seventy-eight, wasn't it?"

"Guess you heard about Clifford? Yeah. Cancer."

I finally managed to get into the house and went into the kitchen. All available counter space was covered with food brought by neighbors and relatives, another custom in West Texas when someone died—make food and bring it to the house so that the grieving family did not have to worry about cooking for all the friends and relatives that would be coming. I filled a paper plate with fried chicken, potato salad, and chocolate chip cookies. I picked up iced tea in what looked to be a jelly jar, and moved out onto the back porch to eat. I saw Charlie sitting at a long table. I sat down beside him.

"How are you doing with this?" I asked. "Losing a brother's got to be tough. You okay?"

Charlie studied me for what seemed to be a long time. It occurred to me that he was considering whether or not we were close enough for an honest answer, and whatever that might reveal, or if a canned reply was safer. Years before we'd been close, but in recent years we'd been little more than casual acquaintances, venturing nothing more than the expected platitudes: "How have you been? How is the family? Good to see you. Let's stay in touch."

To my surprise, he chose honesty.

"It's hard," he said, and paused. Then, "Son and I weren't all that close the last few years, but I loved him. We all knew he could go at any time. His heart wasn't worth a damn, but he wouldn't slow down."

He paused again, studying the food on the plate in front of him, then looked up and said, "But you know what bothers me more than anything else? This is hard to express, but I feel I've lost a connection to Daddy. Son and Daddy were always the closest. Son tried to be Daddy, cowboy and all. When I looked at Son I saw Daddy. I liked that. I still had Daddy as long as I had Son. There was something there. Now I don't have that, and that's what bothers me the most."

He turned back to his plate. I was silent for a moment, thinking of what had just happened. I had expected the usual mindless platitudes, but this was very different. Part of me wanted to play it safe, but I felt I owed him an honest response, even if it did make me uncomfortable. I took a drink of jelly-jar tea and looked out through the screen covering of the porch toward Twin Peaks as I thought about what he had said.

"You know, I hadn't really thought about it that way," I said. "But you're right. In a way, Son was a connection between all of us and our fathers. They were all cowboys and none of us were, except Son. He was a link back to when our dads were alive, and we were kids. Now that's gone, and we're more removed from our fathers than before. I need to think about that; I'm not sure how I feel about it."

"What are you two old farts whispering about?" Robert Earl asked as he sat down across the table from us, sitting down a paper plate of fried chicken and pecan pie. He also had a jelly glass filled with iced tea. "You look pretty serious."

"Charlie just made a very good point, and I'm mulling over the implications."

"Anything you can share?"

I looked at Charlie, who shrugged, leaving it up to me. I decided to share.

"We were talking about how Son was a link between us and our dads. He did what they all dreamed of doing, he cowboy'd. In a way, he followed in their footsteps for all of us. Charlie said he always saw his father in Son, and that Son's death separates him even farther from his father. I didn't realize it till Charlie explained it, but I think I have some of the same feelings. We all lost the last connection to our fathers by losing Son."

Robert Earl put down his fork. He put his hands in his lap and looked out the screen as I had done. His eyes slowly watered as he sat motionless and silent, thinking. For the first time I noticed that he looked thinner than I remembered, and pale. Or maybe not. It had been a long time since I'd seen him. Maybe he'd always been this pale and thin.

"I think you're right," Robert Earl said after several minutes. "I think that may be what's been bothering me, but I didn't really get what it was. Son and I haven't been close since we were kids, and I barely saw him in the last few years, but I've felt really bad about his death, more so than I thought I should. I think you may have just explained it to me."

We sat silently, thinking. Moved, but also embarrassed at the deep feelings we'd shared. It was an awkward silence.

Billy Rex joined us at the table with a paper plate of food. "Damn," he said, "I'd forgotten we had so many relatives that are still alive. I haven't seen most of these people in years."

He took a drink of iced tea. "I haven't had any great desire to see some of these people, but it is nice to see Aunt Ida and Aunt Vera. Hard to believe Granny Myrtle's still alive. I stopped to say hello to her, and she didn't have a clue who I was."

"I need to stop and visit with her too," I said. "I doubt she'll remember me either. Hell! If I make it to ninety-two I just want to remember to breathe and eat every day."

"And poop," Charlie added. "Never underestimate the value of a good bowel movement every day. A good BM every day will keep the doctor away. Forget that nonsense you've heard about apples. Regularity is the key to long life."

"I'll remember to ask Granny Myrtle if she's had a good bowel movement today."

"Guess Tommy told you guys about last night's exploits?" Billy Rex said with glee.

"We don't need to talk about that," I quickly put in, but it was too late.

"What are you talking about?" Charlie asked, and Robert Earl also queried, "What's the story? Tell us."

"You want to tell them or do you want me to?" Billy Rex asked, delighted.

"I'll do it," I said. "Might as well get it over with." And I told the story of my previous evening's truck murder. By the time I finished all three were laughing heartily.

"That's a great story!" Robert Earl said finally. "But I want to know, are you really going to mount the grill over your mantle?" And the three of them started laughing again.

Hearing the laughter, several relatives came over to see what was so funny. My three cousins delighted in telling the tale of the infamous truck kill. Within minutes I was sure everyone there knew the story. I had to take an aggressive response.

"How many of you would have had the creativity in an emergency to try a bank shot off the hood?" I asked. "Anyone could have shot right at it, but where would the sport be in that? How was I to know Pecos had a defective hood on that old truck? And by the way, that might have been the biggest mountain lion in Texas. He was at least five feet tall at the shoulders." And on and on it went.

"Where are we staying tonight?" Billy Rex asked, changing the subject after they had squeezed every bit of life out of the story.

In spite of the fact that he was in the same town as much of his family,

Charlie said that he also needed a place to spend the night. Roy Don was going to spend the night with Vernon and Starlene, he told us, but Charlie preferred a motel.

"I know," Charlie said, snapping his fingers. "Why don't we go see if we can stay at the old Holland Hotel. That'd really be fun after all these years."

The Holland Hotel was an historic hotel in Alpine, the namesake for Holland Avenue. It had been the center of most town activity in Alpine when we were kids. I didn't even know it was still open, but I remembered a grand place we always walked past in awe, going to and from the Saturday matinees. We agreed to try there first.

When we had finished our lunch we made a tour of the house and yard, trying to make sure we shook the hands of as many relatives as possible. Eventually we made it to the front porch where Granny Myrtle sat rocking in a straight-backed wooden rocking chair. Aunts Ida and Vera had joined her, sitting on a double porch swing.

"Have a seat and visit awhile, boys," Vera said, indicating several chairs around the porch. We pulled chairs over and gathered around the three matrons.

"What are you doing now, Tommy?" she asked me. "Besides killing pickup trucks, I mean?"

"Still running a hospital in Austin," I said, ignoring the truck killing part.

"And you, Billy Rex?"

"Oh I'm still working in a bank Aunt Vera," he said.

"What'd he say?" Ida asked, and Vera loudly repeated what Billy Rex had said.

"And you, Robert Earl?"

"I'm still working for the government in Odessa."

"What about you, Charlie?" She completed the circle.

"I'm developing real estate in Dallas." He said.

"Isn't that amazing," Vera said. "All four of you have jobs, and not a one of you is in prison. When you were kids I figured you'd all be locked up by now. I never saw a meaner bunch of boys. Sounds like Tommy still is."

She made a show of winking at Ida as we laughed.

"Looks like rain!" Granny Myrtle exclaimed loudly.

"How are you doing, Grandmother Myrtle?" I asked her, raising my voice for her to hear. "I haven't seen you in years. You look good."

"I'm pretty bad off," she moaned. "Don't think I've got much time left before the good Lord calls me home."

"You're too goddamn mean to die," snorted Ida. "And if I were you, I wouldn't be too sure about the Lord being the one to make the call."

"Ida!" Vera exclaimed, shocked.

"Oh, kiss off Vera," Ida said.

We laughed as we enjoyed the act between the two sisters that we had all heard many times before.

"Grandmother Myrtle," I said, "you've seen a lot and done a lot in ninety-two years. Is there anything you regret not doing, or anything you'd like to do again?"

"Well," she said slowly, "I guess there is one thing I'd like to do again."

"What's that?" I asked.

"I'd like to have an orgasm."

"Myrtle!" Vera exclaimed. "What are you thinking, talking like that?"

"He asked, so I told him."

"Well I never!" Vera said again, flustered.

"Yes you did," retorted Ida. "Don't forget I used to double date with you."

"Ida!" Vera almost shouted. "Don't you go telling lies like that!"

"Lies! Lies! I can still remember you howling in the back seat when we were eighteen. 'Oh God! Oh God! Oh Raaaaaaandy!'"

I was stunned at the response my question had prompted, not sure what to do or say, so I just sat there with my mouth hanging open. Billy Rex almost choked trying to hold back laughter, but Charlie and Robert Earl were howling.

"I will not sit here and be made a fool of!" Vera rose from the swing seat and stomped off the porch.

"God already did that, sweetie," called Ida. "I'm just pointing it out."

"I still think it's going to rain," Granny Myrtle said. She was unaware of the absurdity of the moment.

"Let's go see if there's room for us at the hotel," I said as I rose from my chair. Billy Rex, Robert Earl, and Charlie followed, the three of them still laughing at the scene I had created. We said our goodbyes to Ida and Grandmother Myrtle and departed.

"I guess I'll know never to ask her an open-ended question like that again." I sighed as we crossed the street.

"I don't know," Charlie deadpanned. "But I sort of heard that as an invitation. I think she's sweet on you."

Chapter 21

I drove back to the church so that Billy Rex could retrieve his car, and he followed me to the hotel on Holland Avenue, in the center of town. The hotel took up most of an entire block on the north side of the street. It was a three-story building—the first floor was brick, and the two upper floors were stucco facade. A portico roof supported by two large columns extended from above the front entrance, covering the sidewalk to the street. I remembered walking past that entrance on the way to the movie theater, located only three blocks farther down Holland Avenue. I remembered walking beneath the roof over the sidewalk and peeking through the front door of the hotel. At that time in my life I thought it must have been the grandest, richest, nicest place anywhere. Ceiling fans inside pushed air from a shoeshine stand, a restaurant, and a barbershop out the door—a fragrant mixture of the aromas of shoe polish, food, aftershave, and scented hair tonic. As I drove past the front entrance, I experienced the smell of the hotel forty years ago for a brief instant. I wondered if those same great, exotic smells still came floating out the door.

After parking in an unpaved parking lot to the west side of the hotel, I walked around to the front door and saw that the hotel was neither as large nor as grand as I'd remembered; its age was showing. Nonetheless, it was still a historic landmark, and an important memory from my youth.

The hotel restaurant that had been the source for some of the great aromas I remembered was gone, an empty space now. The shoeshine stand and barbershop were also gone. The only thing that remained as I remembered was a small bar that had been to the right of the front door. It was still there, and appeared not to have changed at all.

Charlie, Robert Earl, and Billy Rex arrived as I stood in front of the hotel, remembering. We entered the hotel together. Stairs led upward on the right, and an ancient elevator sat waiting. Emerging from the entry hallway, we saw why the old restaurant on the street was no longer in use. The entire lobby of the old hotel had been turned into a restaurant. We stood confused for a moment, trying to get our bearings.

"What the hell is this?" I asked, wondering if the hotel of my youth no longer existed.

"Looks like a damn north Dallas fern bar," replied Robert Earl, distaste dripping from his words.

Billy Rex noticed a building directory next to the lonesome elevator. "Here we go," he said. "Look at this."

We saw that while the first floor was now a restaurant, and the second floor now offices, there was still a Holland Hotel in operation. The hotel office was on the second floor with the other offices, but the third floor was designated as guest rooms.

"Thank God," I sighed. "I was starting to get really depressed."

"Well let's go see what's up there before you get undepressed," Charlie said as he headed for the stairs.

We climbed the two flights of stairs to the second floor and easily located the Holland Hotel Office and Building Management, surrounded by several real estate offices. Following Charlie into the room we came upon a middle-aged lady occupying one of several desks in the office.

"May I help you?" she cheerfully asked as we entered.

"We'd like to spend the night here, we think," said Charlie. "Is this place still a hotel?"

"Oh yes," she replied. "We don't get as much business as in the old days, so we've rented out a lot of the space in the building. But we've kept the third floor as a hotel and try to keep it as close as possible to the way it was in its prime. If you like old historic buildings, you will love it here. How many rooms do you want?"

"Four if you have them," Charlie said.

"Well," the lady said to me. "Since you are the tallest I'll put you in 308. It has extra long beds, and you look like you will need one." She then assigned Billy Rex to 310, Robert Earl to 312, and Charlie to 316. We each filled out the requisite registration documents and climbed up one more flight of stairs to the third floor. We were arrayed across the front of the hotel, each of us with a view out onto Holland Avenue.

Room 308 was a rather small, but comfortable hotel room. There were two twin beds with a nightstand between. I immediately noticed that there was no telephone in the room. The bathroom had an antique-looking pedestal sink, a commode with a wooden handled pull chain hanging from an elevated water tank, and an antique bathtub. While the sleeping room looked to have been updated, the bathroom reminded me of the historic hotel I remembered. A wave of nostalgic euphoria elevated my mood.

I took the old elevator back to the first floor and walked to my truck to retrieve my bag and my cell phone. Staying in a room without a phone had its nostalgic charm, but I needed contact with the outside world. Back in the room, I changed into khaki trousers and an oxford shirt. In my Hush Puppies I hardly looked cowboy, but would not look so out of place as in the business suit I had worn to the funeral.

Just as I was leaving the room to meet my cousins for the wake, shrill beeps erupted from my pager. Glancing at the screen, I saw that *hospital administration* was demanding a return call. I thought briefly of ignoring the summons, but habit and culture were too strong. With a sense of dread, my euphoria quickly dissipating, I sat on the bed and dialed the number.

Robert Blake answered before the second ring. "Tom? I've got Paul Jordan here, so I'm putting you on speaker phone." Paul Jordan, an Austin bank president, was chairman of the hospital's board of directors. His presence at the hospital on a Saturday meant *something* significant was going on.

"Tom," Paul immediately took over the conversation, "Robert has briefed me on the situation here, and I'm very concerned. When can we expect you back?" The implication was that I should either already be on my way back to the hospital, or begin driving in that direction immediately.

"What *situation* are we talking about Paul?" I asked.

"The crisis with the obstetricians!"

"I'm not aware of a crisis," I answered wearily. "A group of our physicians wants the hospital to spend millions in hospital money on a project that will line their pockets, but would be financially devastating for the hospital. I've told them I can't support that. When the board hears the financial projections on Monday, they'll feel the same way. It's a boondoggle, Paul."

"Of course it's a boondoggle! What else would you expect from a bunch of doctors? But you know you can't just tell them 'no.' They're like spoiled children—tell them 'no,' they'll throw a tantrum. In this case the tantrum could mean taking their patients to the competition."

There it was—the constant fear of hospital boards—that the physicians might withhold admissions. I suspected that fear had been stoked by Robert Blake.

"Paul, you know they're not going to do that." I talked slowly, trying not to lose my temper. "My God! The whole OB staff is in our office building. They will not drive across Austin to deliver at the Columbia hospital and then drive back across Austin to our site for office visits. They might threaten to do that—maybe even try it for a week or so—but they will give it up once it begins to slightly inconvenience them."

"Even a week's worth of lost revenue would hurt us," said the board chairman, fear evident in his voice. "We're barely making budget now. Losing any revenue will be damned painful, and if these assholes get in a snit it could spread to other members of the medical staff."

"Paul, would you really want me to support a project that would be disastrous for the hospital just to avoid conflict with a few doctors?"

"Hell, we don't have to actually *do* it! Let's just say we need to study it more—stall for time. Maybe we can come up with something else they want, buy them off." What he really meant was that if the conflict could be avoided at this time it might come to a head when someone else was board chairman, and he would not have to deal with it.

"That's dishonest," I said. "And when they realize we've lied to them, we'll have a *real* crisis on our hands. Why not just show some courage and get this over with?"

"This isn't a good time for a confrontation with the doctors," said Paul. "When are you coming back so we can talk about this?"

"I'll be back in Austin sometime Sunday night," I answered, surprising myself. I clearly understood his implied command for me to get back immediately.

"I thought you were supposed to be back tonight or early Sunday." The board chairman sounded surprised at my response. "I'm here at the hospital, and so is Robert. I damn well think you should be here too!"

"Paul, would you take me off the speaker and pick up the phone please," I asked, not wanting Robert to hear. I was working hard to control my growing anger.

I listened to the click and the obvious change in tone as he made our conversation a private one.

"Paul," I began, taking pains to talk slowly and carefully, "I've been doing a lot of thinking on this trip, and I've decided I have taken all the crap I am going to take. I've done the right thing here, and you know it. My job is to protect the hospital's assets, not make a bunch of asshole doctors any richer than they already are. If the board won't back me on this, then you'd better think about firing me. With my contract, that means paying me for a year after I'm gone. Right now, I'd be happy to take my year's pay and ride off into the sunset. Sooner or later, someone has to stand up for what's right."

"Now don't go giving me that cowboy bullshit. Slow down and think carefully," Paul said in a conciliatory tone. "It's clear you're upset, but this is not something worth throwing away your career over. Let's just think about it tonight, and talk about it tomorrow. Let's not do anything rash." It was clear that this conversation had created far more controversy than he was prepared to deal with.

I agreed with his suggestion to delay my decision, more as a way to end the conversation than any real agreement, and we hung up. Tossing the cell phone aside and rising from the bed, feeling a bit light-headed and nauseous, I went into the bathroom and splashed cold water on my face, then went back and sat on the bed to think about what I'd just done.

There was a knock at the door, and I could hear Billy Rex ask from the hall outside my doorway, "Tom. Do you want to ride with us to the wake? We are all going together."

"I've got a couple of calls to make first," I replied. "You guys go on ahead. I'll catch up with you there?"

"Okay," Billy Rex said. "See you there."

I listened to the sounds of the three of them moving to the elevator. I heard the elevator arrive on our floor, heard them talking as they loaded on the elevator, and then it was silent on the third floor.

I lay back on the bed, my hands behind my head, and let out a slow sigh as I closed my eyes. I thought back to my conversation with Paul Jordan. In my whole career, I had never been so rebellious and abrupt with a board member, much less the president, even though there had been many occasions when I literally bit my tongue to keep from telling one how I really felt.

"Don't give me a bunch of that cowboy bullshit," Paul had said. What had I said? After a moment's thought I recalled saying something about standing up for what was right, and riding off into the sunset. Was that what he thought of as cowboy shit, I wondered. Whatever he thought of it, I couldn't believe I had actually said that. What had made me say that? Was it coming back to Alpine, and the cowboy funeral, or memories of Jim Cobb, and my father, and of Lash LaRue?

Suddenly I had a delicious fantasy of having Lash's bullwhip and popping it on Robert Blake's ass! I had no doubt that Robert had agitated the situation at the hospital, and the thought of him running from me holding his ass as I ran along popping the bullwhip on his behind made me feel much better.

Why am I sitting here giggling when I'm about to get my ass fired? I wondered, but even as I asked the rhetorical question I knew this was something that had been building within me. In truth, I thought about it every morning, after another sleepless night, when I climbed out of bed and forced myself to go to the hospital. I hated what I was doing—dealing with greedy, egotistical doctors, and being part of the hypocrisy of an industry that made huge amounts money off human suffering, while bragging shamelessly about the goodness of our supposedly charitable mission. However, always up to this point, before I got too far into those thoughts, I always remembered the very nice salary and lifestyle, which I had always judged to be an acceptable trade-off, and kept my mouth shut. This time I had stuck my foot in my mouth without hesitation.

My mind wandered back to the impressive funeral I had attended for Son. I wondered how many of the doctors that I had been trying to keep happy would come to my funeral if I dropped dead tomorrow? Not too many, unless they thought they could give their condolences to my widow and bill the insurance company for grief counseling. Or board members. None of them would read a poem for me or sing a sad song for me. Sure as hell none of them would ride a horse for me, and the thought of our prissy, spoiled doctors trying to ride a horse made me laugh again.

I lay on the bed for some time. Daydreaming of whipping Robert Blake's ass with Lash LaRue's whip and of our effete physicians falling off horses was some sort of a defense mechanism. It kept me from dwelling too hard on the real question—why I was so damned unhappy, and what was I going to do about it? I decided to pull a Scarlet O'Hara—"I'll worry about this tomorrow"—and left for the wake.

Chapter 22

The Casa Blanca was a combination Mexican restaurant, bar, and dance hall. An Alpine landmark, it was frequented by an eclectic mix of cowboys, college students, and townspeople. It was generally referred to simply as the Casa.

The restaurant was located one block south of the railroad tracks that divided the town, in a sort of cultural neutral zone. Alpine was split in half by the railroad in more ways than just geographically. North of the tracks was the Anglo portion of the town, and the traditionally Mexican area was on the south side. These divisions evolved at a time when Texas was still a segregated society, when many of the same prejudices toward blacks in other parts of the country existed for Mexicans in Texas. Those prejudices and separations had not disappeared entirely, but they had been greatly diluted or blurred in recent years. Old customs died slowly, and the majority of Anglos still lived to the north and Mexicans to the south of the railroad tracks, though now as much from habit and preference as from societal pressures.

The Casa was a large, white, wood-frame building. A red neon sign above the front door identified CASA BLANCA in script lettering. Entering the front door put me in the restaurant, a wood-floored room taking up roughly one third of the building. Metal chairs surrounded metal tables with well-used Formica tops. The kitchen was to the rear of the restaurant section, and as I walked in I was immediately besieged by the pungent scents of chilis, fried meat, tortillas, and assorted Mexican spices. The sharp aromas reminded me that I was hungry. I wove my way through the tables of relaxed diners into the bar and dancehall.

Passing through the door from the restaurant I was enveloped by a cacophony of noise. Just past the door, a wide mahogany bar stretched the width of the room, complete with a brass foot rail that was currently supporting the boots of a dozen or so cowboys standing at the bar. Two bartenders were working furiously to keep up with demand, rapidly filling drink orders that were loudly delivered by several waitresses and the cowboys at the bar.

At the opposite end of the room was the bandstand. The cowboy band that had sung at the funeral occupied the bandstand. As I entered they were executing a furiously energetic rendition of "Cotton-Eyed Joe." An enthusiastic group of dancers was engaged in line-dancing to the song on the dance floor between the bar and bandstand. The tune and its communal dance are a Texas tradition that fills any dance floor in the state. The crowd was almost completely cowboy. Most of the male dancers wore hats, as well as jeans and boots, and almost all the women wore jeans and boots, but no hats.

The dancers were moving rapidly as a single unit—almost as cohesive as a military drill team—in a huge counter clockwise circle on the floor. The laughing and whooping of the dancers, mixed with the sounds from the bar and the music from the band, resulted in a din so intense and powerfully joyful as to be irresistible.

On each side of the room flanking the dance floor, tables and chairs of the same variety as those in the restaurant were crowded against the walls. The walls themselves were covered with pictures of Willie Nelson, Waylon Jennings, George Strait, and other country singing stars; Frederick Remington and Charles Russell western art prints; old posters of Roy Rogers, Gene Autry, and Tom Mix movies; and old tin beer signs advertising Lonestar, Pearl, and Pabst Blue Ribbon. There were branding irons, spurs, and even pieces of several varieties of barbed wire also attached to the walls.

With most of the crowd on the dance floor, it was easy to spot my cousins. Billy Rex, Robert Earl, Starlene and her husband Vernon, Roy Don, and Charlie occupied three tables they had pulled together into a single unit. An impressive array of empty beer bottles already littered the tables where they sat. My cousins had not wasted any time getting into the spirit of a wake.

Between Starlene and Roy Don was an empty chair with a white hat hanging on the back. I recognized the hat as Son Cable's hat, the one that had been laying on his chest at the funeral.

Billy Rex and Robert Earl were dressed in non-western outfits similar to my own—khaki trousers and long-sleeved cotton shirts open at the collar. Robert Earl wore a red and blue checkered shirt while Billy Rex had on a navy blue shirt. Charlie continued to be fashionably correct in boots, jeans, and a tan western-style shirt. Roy Don and Vernon wore boots, jeans, and the pale blue denim work shirts normally worn by working men in this part of the world. Only Vernon wore a western hat. Starlene wore a western-style denim skirt and a white blouse.

All of them were laughing at something. They had not noticed me. I moved to the bar and stood watching them laughing together, a scene reminiscent of our childhood that had not been repeated in recent years. We had scattered throughout Texas after that summer, and I thought about the different paths all of us had taken, and the paths that had led us back, as I stood watching my cousins happily talking and laughing at the tables.

Ten of the original twelve cousins were still alive, but we had scattered considerably. Of the five Cable kids, only Son and Starlene had stayed in Alpine. Son had managed to find more or less continuous work as a cowboy—even managing to save enough to buy a small piece of land west of town, near Twin Peaks I understood.

Starlene had married a local boy and they built a house less than a mile from the home where she grew up. Her husband, Vernon, was a solid, good man, and they had raised three children, and lived a quiet life in Alpine. They now had grandchildren.

Roy Don worked for the Texas State Highway Department in San Antonio. He had gone into the army following high school, came back, attended and graduated from Sul Ross, and went to work as an engineer on road construction projects. He was nearing retirement tenure now. His family—a wife and three kids—had not accompanied him on this trip.

Charlie had fulfilled the promise of his youth, developing into a star athlete at both the high school and college levels, and had even enjoyed a brief period of success in professional baseball. He made it to the major leagues and even played in one World Series. The talented Charlie had glided through life being good at almost everything he tried, with little or no effort required on his part. He was a good enough guitar player and singer to have made a couple or records following his professional baseball career. Unfortunately, his singing career ended when his sports notoriety faded and left behind a singer with a good—but not great—voice in an industry filled with great voices. Charlie then drifted into male modeling for several years, until the fresh look of youth began to fade.

Charlie now existed in a perpetual state of adolescence common in former star athletes. In Charlie's case this post-athletic immaturity had been exacerbated by his brief singing career and his turn in the modeling business. Charlie's whole life had been spent as the adored center of attention, which appeared to have left him ill-equipped to deal with anonymity. Fortunately, he had played professional baseball just long enough to qualify for a pension, which he now lived on while pretending to be a high-powered real estate developer. He had used up three marriages and found himself alone now in his fifties. He occupied himself playing in small-town celebrity golf tournaments that featured old athletes. Although he often had to explain to his playing partners who he was, or had been, it gave him the opportunity to continue playing the role of the hero—the only role life had really prepared him to play.

Dad Cable died of a heart attack in 1977 while horseback riding alone at Son's place. Everyone who knew him thought it was a good death for an old cowboy. Arva had died in 1988, so Starlene and Vernon's oldest daughter and her family lived in the old Cable house now.

My father's brother Ray had not been so lucky as to die a cowboy's death. He had wasted away and died of cancer in 1979, an empty husk of a human being suffering horribly in a lonely hospital bed. Robert Earl had never officially come out of the closet. After finishing high school in Pecos, Texas, Robert Earl had gone on to The University of Texas at Austin and majored in social work. He now worked for the Texas Workers' Compensation Commission in El Paso. He had never formed any type of lasting relationship that I knew of, male or female. His sister Aloe had not come to the funeral. Blossom did, but had happily driven back to Fort Stockton immediately afterward to work the night shift at the Firestone tire testing plant outside Fort Stockton.

Dewayne was killed in a car wreck while still in his teens. Billy Rex had been riding with him, and was severely injured. He eventually recovered, graduated from Sul Ross, and went on to a career in banking.

My father passed away in 1978. He had never gotten back to ranch work, although he still had dreams and plans to do so up till the moment he died. My mother was still living. She had remarried and lived in Odessa with Sissy, who worked as the manager for a motel on the freeway through town.

Following that memorable summer in Alpine my family had moved around West Texas for several years chasing construction jobs until my mother had finally insisted on settling in one spot. After high school I went on to Sul Ross on a football scholarship. After college I taught school and coached football for several years. Then, after marriage, I went back to Trinity University in San Antonio for a master's degree in health care administration that qualified me for and eventually led me to my current job in Austin.

As I stood at the bar thinking about life since our summer together, Billy Rex noticed me and waved for me to come over. I wove my way through the dancers and tables to their location. The men all stood to shake my hand and Starlene gave me a big hug while saying, "I'm *so* glad you came. It's been so long since we've seen you." Starlene was a tall woman, around five feet eight and slightly heavy, with brown hair cut shoulder length. With her air of confidence and authority, she was still the mother figure for all of us. Vernon was an average-sized man with prematurely gray hair, and a kind, wizened face. He had the solid appearance of a man who had done hard work all his life, as indeed he had. When we shook hands the calluses on his hand felt like rough wood. Vernon was one of the most congenial men I had ever known though, and as always, his weathered face was creased by a wide friendly smile.

"Hey partner!" Charlie gushed as he grasped my hand and flashed a toothy smile. "Where have you been? We were starting to worry about you. You have to take care of some business in that hospital in Austin?"

"Yeah," I replied. "A few things came up I had to attend to."

"Well, we need to talk later," Charlie said. "I've got some deals cooking up that way you might be interested in."

"Sure," I agreed. Charlie seemed to have discarded the honesty of our earlier conversations and become the dealmaker.

Turning to Roy Don, whom I had not been able to talk with at the funeral, I said, "Roy Don, it's been a really long time since I've seen you. What have you been up to?" Roy Don's hair was still red, though speckles of gray were beginning to appear. A little on the short side—about five foot eight inches—Roy Don was a stout man. Working in the sun for years had given his face a permanent sunburn. Although he had been a hyperactive kid, Roy Don had become quiet almost to the point of being withdrawn as an adult, silent and thoughtful.

"Oh, just building highways. Same old stuff," he said in reply, simple and direct as always.

"Are you still in San Antonio?" I asked.

"Yes. Still there," he answered.

After I had greeted everyone, we filled each other in on our jobs, our kids, and our spouses. Charlie only had one kid, a son by his first marriage, and I learned that he was now attending Texas Tech University. I was surprised to hear that both of Roy Don's sons had already graduated from college. One was a county extension agent in southern Texas, and the other was teaching school in San Antonio. Starlene's children had also finished school, and all were now married and raising families of their own. Billy Rex and I had kids still in high school, while Robert Earl had no children.

"Do you guys remember," Robert Earl said, during a lull in the conversation, "when we used to all get together as one big huge family when we were kids? We used to go camping together and stuff like that. It was almost like a family reunion every time we all got together. I really miss that, all the uncles and aunts and cousins, really being a *family*."

"Son said almost exactly the same thing a few months ago," Starlene said. "He was over at our house for supper one Sunday, and he got to talking about all the things we did as kids, and how sorry he was that we all weren't close any more."

"That reminds me," I interrupted her. "Is that Son's hat there on that chair?"

"Yes," she answered, and we all looked at the hat on the empty chair. "His friends wanted him to be here in some way tonight, so they decided to keep an empty chair for him, and put his hat on it to show it was his seat. They said they were going to put the hat somewhere in here to keep after the party."

At that moment a cowboy approached our table, his hat in his hands in a gesture of respect. A pretty, blonde cowgirl accompanied him. "I guess you folks are Son's family?" the man asked. "I only know Vernon and Star." He held out his hand to each of the rest of us sitting at the table, introducing himself as Bill Hightower. His hand was hard and rough in the same manner as Vernon's, and his grip was well beyond firm.

"I worked with Son on several of the ranches around here. He was a good hand, and I counted him as a friend. You could depend on him for help if you needed it. He'd always be the first one to volunteer to help some neighbor with branding, or any other work that needed doing. I'm proud to have been his friend, and I'm going to miss him." The recitation brought tears to the eyes of the rough-looking cowboy, and the girl stepped forward and put her arm around him.

"Anyway," Bill concluded, "I just wanted to pay my respects to you folks." He turned and moved away, reaching into his back pocket for a handkerchief, the girl still holding him tightly.

I realized my own eyes were tearing up, and most of the men at the table were sniffing loudly while Starlene wiped her eyes with a handkerchief supplied by Vernon. It was a touching scene I had not been prepared for. And it was just the first of many. Over the next two hours it seemed as if every cowboy in the house made a similar appearance at our table to pay his respects to the family. Each removed his hat before approaching, and told stories of Son being a good neighbor or friend, of his willingness to help others in need, and of his love for the land and the cowboy life. I learned about my deceased cousin's life, and the more I heard the more I admired and respected him.

"Son came over and worked for about two weeks on my place one spring when my leg was busted and I couldn't afford no help. And he wouldn't take nothing for it neither, even after I got ahead later. Said that's what friends was supposed to do."

"Son helped me dig the well at my folk's house one summer. Damn it was hot, but he came over every evening, and we would work for two or three hours on that well. Said all he wanted in return was a cold Lone Star when we quit each day. I confess we drank more than one on most days though."

"When my boy was playing football for the high school, Son went to every game with me, even when it was colder than the devil. I remember one night over in Marfa when it froze and sleeted the whole game, but he sat up there in those metal stands with me. He didn't care nothing about football, but my wife and I had just separated and he said I didn't need to be travelin' around alone. He just went to keep me company."

After a while, as cowboy after cowboy came to our table and told of his relationship with Son, I began to get a fair perception of his life. Son had unwaveringly pursued a cowboy life. He had inherited whatever strange gene it is that makes a man want to work his ass off in a profession that some have described as providing the lowest of compensation, while demanding the highest level of skill, to work in some of the worst working conditions, of any profession available to man. But at the same time that profession offered a man a greater sense of freedom and self-reliance than was available in other pursuits, and a sense of self-satisfaction at the end of each day of having actually done something with his own hands, something that could be seen and touched. Son lived by a code of conduct that stressed the value of hard work, honesty, respect for others and for the country, and the value of and necessity for being a good neighbor in a country where neighbors were often few and far between. It was a profession where success is not measured as much by how much a man accumulates, as by how good a man he is.

More than the rest of us, Son had listened to our cowboy uncles and fathers talk lovingly of the joys of the cowboy life, heard them sing the old cowboy songs. As I thought back, I realized he had been a cowboy in his heart by the time he was ten years old. I wondered for a moment why it was that none of the rest of the seven boy cousins had taken that path, had inherited that gene?

I gradually became aware again of hunger. I ordered some border eggs—corn tortillas covered first with a piece of white cheese, then a round piece of yellow cheese about the size of a silver dollar in the middle with a slice of jalapeno pepper underneath. The whole thing was put into the oven until the cheeses have melted into one another. What came out looked like a fried egg—round, flat, and white with a smaller yellow center—but tasted fantastic, and the jalapeno in the center generated reflexive grabbing for cold beer, or any other liquid. The border eggs arrived eight on a platter. We shared the first order, eagerly sucked down all the beer left on the table, and ordered more of both.

In between eating eggs and listening to the cowboys who came by to pay their respects, we began to reminisce and share stories about one another. I found myself the object of several of these stories.

"Do you guys remember," Charlie asked, laughing before even telling the story, "when Tommy used his sister's foot to kill the spider?" As they talked about me as a child each of the cousins reverted to calling me "Tommy" rather than the "Tom" I had become as an adult.

"We were all just babies when this happened. I guess Tommy was about three or four, and Sissy was still in a walker. They were over at our house one night, and a big old daddy longlegs spider came crawling across the floor. Uncle Tom told Tommy to stomp it, kill it, but he didn't want any part of that spider. Just about that time Sissy came pushing by in her walker, so Tommy grabbed her, pushed the walker over to the spider, picked up Sissy's bare foot, and used it to stomp the spider! You could hear Sissy scream all over Alpine. The spider didn't hurt her, just scared her, and she screamed and cried, and Tom gave Tommy one hell of a whipping."

We all laughed at the story. "Well that seems pretty smart to me," Billy Rex said. "You used the tools on hand to do the job."

"I wish my daddy had seen it that way," I said.

"Every time we all get together," Charlie said—meaning his brothers and sisters more than the rest of us—"we tell the story about when Tommy used his sister's foot to kill a spider."

"Good Lord!" Starlene exclaimed, laughing. "I don't see how Sissy survived to grow up with you as her brother. I remember when you shot her from the outhouse with your BB gun."

Both Billy Rex and Robert Earl said that they didn't remember hearing about that, and prodded me to tell the story.

"Well," I started, "this was when I was five I think, and Sissy would have been three. We were visiting the Cables, and all of us had driven out in the country to visit Granny Myrtle. She had an old one-seater outhouse out back of her house. We were all playing and everything, hunting lizards with our BB guns, when I had to go real bad. I went in and latched the door and settled down to do my business. After I had just gotten started Sissy came up and started banging on the door and hollering that she had to go. I told her to go away, but she just kept beating on the door and screaming for me to get out because she had to go. She was interrupting my concentration and spoiling my movement, and it got annoying as hell. She wouldn't go away. Finally, I noticed that the door on the outhouse had about four inches clearance at the bottom, and I could see Sissy's bare feet as she pounded on the door and continued to shriek. I'd taken my BB gun into the outhouse with me and had it leaning against the wall in the corner. I grabbed it, held the muzzle about six inches from Sissy's big toe, and pulled the trigger. I shot her dead center on the toenail of her big toe. I'm sure you all remember how much it hurt to get shot with a BB gun from close range. Imagine how it felt on your big toe nail from six inches.

"Well Sissy's foot immediately disappeared from under the door, and you could hear her scream clear to Fort Stockton. Of course she peed all over herself, and ran around hopping on one foot and screaming. She eventually lost the toenail on that toe. I stayed in the outhouse hiding for a long time, but when I finally came out my daddy was waiting for me with his belt off. Man! He whipped my butt for that! Took my BB gun away from me for about a month too. That was the worst thing."

Everyone at the table was laughing hard, picturing Sissy hopping around the outhouse holding her foot and peeing on herself. "Man, you were mean to your sister!" Robert Earl exclaimed. "It *is* a wonder she ever grew up with you as a brother."

"No! No!" I said, defending myself. "I just had to go, and to this day I get mean and angry when someone interrupts me on the john. So all of you keep that in mind if I have to go tonight!"

"Now isn't there some sort of story like that about the scar Sissy has between her eyes?" Billy Rex asked.

"No. Not like that. That was entirely different," I said. "That time I was trying to protect her." And I went on to explain.

"We were out playing in the chicken pen one day. I guess I was six or seven, and Sissy would have been four or five. We had this old rooster that was mean as hell, and he would attack you if he got the chance. He'd try to spur you."

Roosters have thorn-like protrusions on the rear of their legs, just above the feet. These protrusions are called spurs, and roosters use them to fight. The spurs were enhanced with razor-like blades tied to them in cockfights, so that one rooster could actually kill another. A rooster jumped up in the air, holding himself aloft as much as possible by flapping his wings, and pawed at his opponent with his feet, raking them with the spurs. They sometimes attacked humans in this manner too. It was hard for them to do much damage to a human, but I was scared to death of that old rooster as a child.

"Well for some reason that old rooster took after Sissy. She got so scared she just sat down right there in the middle of the chicken pen. The rooster actually jumped up on top of her head and was beating his wings like a helicopter. The thought that flashed into my mind was that he was going to spur her in the eyes, put her eyes out, and he really could've done that."

"She was sitting there on the ground, crying and screaming, trying to put her hands up in protection. I didn't know what to do, but then I remembered that I had my toy cowboy cap pistol in its holster around my waist."

"Now don't tell me you shot the rooster with a cap pistol," Billy Rex laughed.

"No, no." I continued, "I knew better than that, but I decided it would make a good weapon to throw at that damned rooster, to kill him dead. So I pulled out the pistol, took dead aim, and threw it as hard as I could. Just about then Sissy sort of raised up a little higher and my pistol caught her right between the eyes, and knocked her flat on her back. Well her dropping like that and the pistol flying by scared the rooster off. He ran over to the other side of the pen, but Sissy was damn near out cold, and she had a cut between her eyes that left the scar Billy Rex was talking about, and a knot about the size of a baseball. I saved her, but I damn near killed her in the process."

Everyone at the table was laughing and pounding the table in glee.

"You know, you're right Star," I said, "Sissy probably *was* fortunate to survive childhood with me as a brother."

"No," Star said as she tried to stop laughing. "The truth is I think every girl who ever grew up with brothers is lucky to survive. Son and Roy Don and Charlie all did things like that and worse to me and Crystal." And she began to tell us stories of her brothers. In this manner we passed several hours, drinking beer, eating border eggs, telling stories on one another remembered from long ago, and greeting cowboys who came to pay their respects. It was the most pure fun I had had in years.

All the while the band continued to play country and western music, and a goodly portion of the crowd was on the dance floor most of the time. People continued to come by our table to talk. More than a few, when introduced to me, said something like, "So you're the fearless truck killer." If anyone in Alpine had not heard the story I would have been surprised. The good news was that I was going to leave, but Pudgie had to stay and suffer the abuse. But then, I realized, Pudgie would relish the attention.

"Hey!" I heard from behind me. "I hear there's an old Dodge truck terrorizing citizens over in Marfa. I hear there's a bounty on it, and they're looking for someone with the courage to go after it."

I turned to see Pig. "Oh, kiss my ass," I said.

"I would," Pig replied as he sat down next to me at the table, "but it's hard to tell where the ass part stops and the rest of you begins." Pig said his hellos to the rest of the people at the table and offered his condolences. He and I talked for a while.

"Pig," I asked, lowering my voice to a level only he could hear, "Do you think there'd be a teaching job here in Alpine for an old fart who wanted to come back into it after being away for twenty or so years?"

"Hmm," Pig said thoughtfully. "Do you reckon that hypothetical old fart would have kept his teaching certificate from his younger years?"

"Yes. You could assume that," I said as I took a long drink of beer.

"Do you think that fictional old fart might also want to do some coaching?" Pig asked as he took a drink out of the Diet Coke he was carrying. A school administrator could not be seen drinking in public, even at a wake.

"I don't know about that," I answered as I thought about it. "It might be that the game has passed him by since the last time he was involved."

"Shit!" Pig snorted as he laughed. "We're talking football. Not brain surgery."

"Well, maybe," I said. I really had not thought about coaching.

"Well, I know Pecos and Pudgie could use someone with a small measure of common sense to keep them calmed down, and I can always use a teacher. You tell the old fart that if you run into him."

"I'll do that," I answered. "Have you seen Pecos and Pudgie and their better halves tonight?"

"Yeah. They're sitting at a table over near the door. Drinkin' Diet Coke like me. We'll probably hit the trail here in a few minutes. You know how it is with us pillars of the community. We can't stay out and practice debauchery with you debauchers. We have an image to uphold, although I have to say the three of you did a good job of lowering that image last night." And he got up to leave.

"Kiss my ass," I called to him as he left. He waved back over his shoulder.

Just then there was a lull in the singing. The sudden silence made everyone look toward the bandstand.

"Ladies and cowboys," the lead singer in the band shouted into the microphone, "can I have your attention?"

When the crowd quieted down he continued, "We have a celebrity with us tonight. Son's brother Charlie, a former major-league baseball player, is here." He pointed toward our table. Charlie half rose and waved as the crowd applauded.

"Now Charlie also sings and has made some records," the band leader continued. "Maybe we can get him to come up and sing one with us." The crowd applauded and whistled.

Acting as if he were reluctant to take the stage, Charlie milked the crowd for several minutes, and then finally rose out of his chair. As he was getting up he looked back at me and winked. He loved this. He was the hero and the center of attention once more. I was happy for him, and cheered and clapped with the rest.

Charlie went to the bandstand, accepted a guitar from one of the players, and looped the strap over his neck. After a few moments of consultation with band members, Charlie took the place at the microphone, and the band began playing. As they played, Charlie began to sing "Amarillo by Morning," a sad but appealing George Strait song about a down-on-his-luck cowboy on the rodeo circuit.

"Amarillo by morning, up from San Antone.
Everything that I got is just what I got on.
When that sun is high in that Texas sky,
I'll be bucking at the County Fair.
Amarillo by morning, Amarillo I'll be there.

I lost my saddle in Houston, broke my leg in Santa Fe.
Lost my wife and a girlfriend somewhere along the way.
But I'll be looking for eight when they throw that gate,
And I hope that judge ain't blind.
Amarillo by morning, Amarillo's on my mind."

The song was a great choice. It was a sad song that matched the occasion, and most in the crowd could relate to the cowboy in the song. Rodeo cowboys are special among cowboys, the most adept at the skills required by the trade—riding animals that did not want to be ridden, roping animals that did not want to be caught. They put their health and even their lives at risk night after night in competition against other great cowboys, for not much money compared to other professional sports. Rodeo cowboys are respected and admired among working cowboys, not in the manner professional baseball or football players are admired by the general populace, but more in the manner that one would respect someone who had achieved much in one's own profession, like an artist might feel about Van Gogh, or a musician might feel about Beethoven. Rather than playing a game designed solely for entertainment, rodeo cowboys compete in the skills their profession demands every day. Working cowboys understand and relate to rodeo cowboys much more so than the rest of us do to over-paid professional prima donnas in other sports. All cowboys know exactly what it feels like to be thrown off a bucking animal. They know the physical pain and the emotional pain of the rodeo cowboy. And above all else they share the love of a profession done not just for the money.

"Amarillo by morning, up from San Antone,
Everything that I got is just what I got on.
I ain't got a dime, but what I've got is mine.
I ain't rich but Lord I'm free.
Amarillo by morning, Amarillo's where I'll be.
Amarillo by morning, Amarillo's where I'll be."

Charlie finished the song to enthusiastic applause and shouts for more. I had forgotten how good Charlie was, almost good enough to sing for a living. And he clearly enjoyed it. He looked as if twenty years had dropped off him as he beamed in the spotlight and the applause.

Holding up his hands to quiet the crowd, Charlie agreed to do another song, and after a few minutes' consultation with the band he sang another George Strait song called "All My Exes Live in Texas," a tongue-in-cheek tale of a cowboy on the run from his ex-wives and sweethearts. The lighthearted nature of the song was a perfect transition from the sad nature of the previous song. Charlie was working the crowd—taking them from mood to mood.

"All my exes live in Texas.
And Texas is the place I'd dearly love to be.
But all my exes live in Texas,
And that's why I hang my hat in Tennessee."

Charlie finished and left the stage to very enthusiastic applause. He had a hard time working his way back to our table through a crowd that wanted to embrace him. He even had to sign several autographs along the way. Finally, he reached our table and sat down. Taking a long drink out of his beer he put it back down on the table and said, "Goddamn I'm good!"

The rest of us laughed, cheered, and agreed with him. "Damn right you're good," I said.

"You're the man!" Billy Rex laughed, holding up his beer in toast, and we all joined in.

By this time in the evening all of us had consumed a considerable number of beers, and were feeling very loose—laughing and having a good time.

"Before I forget," Starlene said, waving her hands to get all our attention, "I need all of you to do something for me. I need you all to meet me at Son's house in the morning."

"I don't know, Star," I said. "I really need to get back. I was planning on leaving pretty early in the morning." Robert Earl and Billy Rex expressed similar concerns.

"I wouldn't ask if it wasn't important," Starlene said earnestly as she leaned forward to show her seriousness. "It's important that we all be there."

"What's this about?" Billy Rex asked, putting down his beer, looking intently at her.

"I'll tell you in the morning," Starlene said. "But it has to do with Son and something he asked me to do. I told him I would."

With the camaraderie, cheer, and goodwill from the eventful day we had experienced, it was impossible to say no. All of us agreed to come, with protestations that we could not stay long and had to get home. We agreed to meet at Son's house at nine-thirty in the morning.

"Ladies and cowboys," the band leader said, diverting our attention. "We need to do something now. Could everyone gather around the family table?"

The crowd moved into sort of a semicircle around our table, and the band leader came over. He had picked up a hammer and a long nail from somewhere on the bandstand. As he approached our table, Red Odell, the cowboy who had read the poem at the funeral, took them from him and silenced the crowd by holding his hand aloft.

"We all hate to let ol' Son go," Red said loudly as the crowd quieted down. "So we decided to keep a part of him with us. We're going to keep his hat here in the Casa to keep his memory alive. We figured the best thing to do was just nail it to the wall with all the rest of the stuff up there, and it'll be there as long as this is a cowboy bar. Charlie, would you like to do the honor?"

Charlie stood and took the hat, hammer, and nail from Red. I noticed a change in Charlie as he took his brother's hat in his hands. Clearly touched, he became somber and respectful as he took his older brother's hat. He turned to the wall, searched for a moment for the appropriate place, and chose the perfect spot next to a branding iron and just above some barbed wire.

Placing the hat brim against the wall, Charlie placed the nail directly in back of the crown and hammered it into place. The hat was now a permanent part of the wall.

"Here's to you, Son," Red Odell said in toast as he raised a beer toward the hat. "May you ride a good horse in tall grass in peaceful valleys, while we keep you in our hearts forever."

"Hear, hear," the cowboys echoed.

For a moment the room was quiet, and a feeling of sadness began to seep into the mood, but then the band leader said loudly, "Let's finish off the evening with the cowboy national anthem." This brought enthusiastic cheers from the cowboys. I was not sure what he meant till the band took the stage again and began playing the Willie Nelson-Waylon Jennings classic, "Mamas, Don't Let your Babies Grow up to be Cowboys." Everyone moved onto the dance floor, placed their arms around another's shoulders or otherwise interlocked, and swayed with the music as the band played. Everyone joined in to sing the chorus to the song.

"*Mamas, don't let your babies grow up to be cowboys.*
Don't let them pick guitars and drive them old trucks.
Make them be doctors and lawyers and such.
Mamas, don't let your babies grow up to be cowboys.
They'll never stay home and they're always alone,
Even with someone they love."

Then the band sang the verse while all of us in the crowd listened and swayed together in sort of a group dance of the heart.

"Cowboys ain't easy to love and they're hard to hold on to.
And they'd rather give you a song than diamonds and pearls.
Lone Star belt buckles and old faded Levi's
And each night begins a new day.
You don't understand him, and if he don't die young,
He'll probably just ride away."

"Mamas, don't let your babies grow up to be cowboys.
Don't let them pick guitars and drive them old trucks.
Make them be doctors and lawyers and such.
Mamas, don't let your babies grow up to be cowboys.
They'll never stay home and they're always alone,
Even with someone they love."

"Cowboys like smoky old pool rooms and clear mountain mornings.
Little warm puppies and children and girls of the night.
And them that don't know him won't like him,
And them that do sometimes won't know how to take him.
He ain't wrong he's just different but his pride won't let him
Do things to make you think he's right."

I gradually realized that we were not just reciting the words to a popular song. Every cowboy in the room was singing about himself, and every girl about her boyfriend or husband or father. And I was singing about Son and my father, and Uncle Ben, and Uncle Ray. While the words of the song said not to let them be cowboys, what we pridefully meant was that those who did become cowboys were special indeed. We all joined in on the last chorus.

"Mamas, don't let your babies grow up to be cowboys.
Don't let them pick guitars and drive them old trucks.
Make them be doctors and lawyers and such.
Mamas, don't let your babies grow up to be cowboys.
They'll never stay home and they're always alone,
Even with someone they love."

As the song came to an end, a great cheer erupted from the crowd. The men in the crowd hugged the women and shook hands and slapped the backs of the other men. There was a feeling of good will and camaraderie in the room that was stronger than I had ever felt. I was stunned with the intensity of the feeling, and did not want it to end. I wanted to feel this close to other human beings forever.

It did gradually come to an end, however. The crowd slowly began to break up and drift out into the parking lot. Pickup trucks began to leave. I joined my cousins at the table we had occupied. We all took one last look at our dead cousin's hat hanging on the wall. It was a fitting tribute to the man who had just wanted to be a cowboy. Then we walked out of the dance hall into a night so clear a million stars were visible in the sky. I continued to be amazed at how many stars were visible in the skies of West Texas. I stood in the parking lot and simply looked up in wonder for a few moments. Literally millions of lights of all different intensities shone in the black sky. It was breathtakingly beautiful, and overwhelming in its immensity.

As I finally walked across the parking lot to my truck I thought about what a contradiction it was that—despite coming here for a family member's funeral—this had been one of the best days of my life.

Chapter 23

The drive from the Casa back to the Holland Hotel was less than ten city blocks, back across the railroad tracks and down Holland Avenue, and only took a few moments. Charlie, Robert Earl, Billy Rex, and I arrived back at the hotel almost simultaneously and walked from the parking lot to the front entrance of the hotel together. It was well after midnight, and we appeared to be the last people in Alpine still awake and about. Not a single automobile was on the street. Not a single light illuminated any of the businesses on the street, and only the inside of the entryway of the hotel was lighted. Even without lights though, the stars and the moon provided enough illumination for us to easily navigate.

Still high from the great day I had experienced, I was not ready for bed.

"Hey guys," I said, as we stood looking up at the stars. "Anyone want to walk over to the old depot for a few minutes before we go to bed?" The hotel was directly across the street from the old railroad depot

"That's a hell of an idea," Billy Rex answered. "I haven't been over there since we were kids."

"Why not?" Robert Earl agreed, and started walking in that direction. "I'm too keyed up to sleep anyway."

"I'm game," Charlie said, and we strolled languidly across Holland Avenue, through the parking lot, around to the front of the depot, and up onto the platform.

"My God!" Robert Earl exclaimed as he paced about the platform. "This place is like stepping back in time. It hasn't changed a bit since we were kids. It looks like some kind of a movie set."

While trains still came through Alpine on a regular basis, and Amtrak passenger trains stopped to deposit or pick up passengers, the depot was a relic of an earlier time, not having changed in any substantial way in over fifty years. A wood-frame building, approximately a hundred feet long, parallel to the tracks, it was painted a pale yellow and trimmed in black, a common color combination for railroad stations when train travel was in vogue. On the trackside a roofed platform ran the entire length of the building to facilitate loading or unloading of passengers, mail, or freight. The entrance to the station was in the center of the roofed platform, flanked on either side by wooden, backless benches. Across the railroad tracks, A Mountain loomed darkly in the moonlight above the depot and the city.

Billy Rex was examining schedules and flyers posted on a large and cluttered billboard outside the entrance. The only light on the platform spread weakly from a single light bulb over the entrance door. Inside, the room was dark, and the door was locked. Peering through the windows, we could make out the shapes of benches and counters. I would not have been surprised to see a pot-bellied, wood-burning stove, but if it was there the darkness concealed it.

After several minutes of scanning the notices and advertisements on the bulletin board, Billy Rex said, "I believe some of this stuff has been hanging here since we were kids." He chuckled as he continued reading.

"You know," Charlie said thoughtfully as he walked up and down the platform, "I've always wanted to buy this old building and turn it into some sort of a small shopping mall, like the one in Dallas." I thought of the train station in Dallas that had been renovated into an upscale and trendy shopping mall and tried to picture something like that in Alpine. It did not fit in my mind.

"I'd rather move it somewhere and turn it into a home," Billy Rex said as he moved away from the bulletin board.

"I don't think either of you is going to get his wish," Robert Earl murmured as he cupped his hands around his face and pressed his nose against the darkened window. "It looks like it's still being used, and I think the trains will always have to come through here. You pretty much have to come through here to get from San Antonio or Austin to El Paso. Don't you?"

"I reckon so," Charlie replied as he joined Robert Earl trying to see into the darkened station.

Sitting down on one of the wooden benches, I stretched out my legs, and leaned back against the wall.

"What a day," I spoke aloud, as much to myself though as to the others. "What a remarkable day! This has absolutely been one of the best days of my life."

"Me too," Billy Rex agreed as he sat down on the other bench. "I sure never expected anything like this when I left home." Charlie and Robert Earl came from the window and sat down with us.

Robert Earl and I sat on one bench, he on my left, and Billy Rex and Charlie sat on the bench to our right, Billy Rex closer to us. The four of us sat silently for several moments, looking out at the tracks and A Mountain beyond the tracks, each reflecting on the day.

Robert Earl finally broke the silence. "You know," he said, leaning back and crossing his arms across his chest, "this has been sort of a revelation for me. Charlie, please don't take this wrong, but I've always thought of Son as something of an under-achiever, someone who really didn't accomplish much, working for diddly-squat as a cowboy while the rest of us were off making careers and money. After today, I think he may have had the most satisfying and successful life of any of us."

The rest of us were silent, mulling over what Robert Earl had said.

"I think you may be right," I said. I leaned forward, elbows on knees, my chin resting on my hands. "Earlier today I was wondering what would've happened if I'd been the one who died. Would the people I work with have honored me the way Son's friends honored him? I've been busting my ass for that hospital and those doctors, but I'm not sure a damned one of them would take an hour off for my funeral if I dropped dead in the hall. And the truth is—I don't feel any more love or affection toward them. We're all just showing up there every day to generate income."

The four of us sat quietly for a few moments. Crickets were chirping in the bushes on the opposite side of the tracks. Finally I broke the silence with a question I would not have even thought of asking before today. "Are you guys happy? I mean really happy, with the way your life has turned out?" I asked.

"Yeah, I guess so," Robert Earl replied after a moment, still leaning back against the wall with his arms crossed across his chest. "I mean, things haven't turned out like I thought they would when I was younger, but I'm pretty happy with where I am."

"Most of the time," Billy Rex said after a minute of thinking, lightly bouncing his chin against his thumbs. "I mean, most of the time I'm pretty satisfied." He stood up and walked across the platform to one of the support posts. He leaned against the post, putting his hands in his pockets and looking back at the three of us. "But I guess we all have our moments of thinking what if."

"Well hell yes I'm happy," Charlie said sarcastically, crossing his arms across his chest to go with his crossed legs. "I'm as happy as a pig in shit."

The four of us were silent several minutes, thinking, looking up and down the starlit tracks as if searching for answers. Fireflies streaked tiny trails of light between A Mountain and the station. A dog could be heard barking somewhere in the darkness.

"It's funny how life works out, isn't it?" Robert Earl finally spoke. "Very little has actually turned out the way I thought it would when we were young. Do you guys remember the time we had the horned toad chariot races? We thought we had a great idea, and planned everything out—worked for days building a racecourse and building the chariots, catching just the right horned toad. Then when we had everything perfectly ready, we turned them loose and all hell broke loose. They ran every which direction instead of where we planned, and most of them got stomped to death by the girls.

"Well," he continued, "I've often thought that life was a lot like those chariot races. We have great ideas and make great plans, and then when the starting gun gets fired everything falls apart and doesn't go anything like we think it will. I think we have about as much control over our lives as we had over those horned toads. Life is a horned toad chariot race."

"That's pretty good," I answered, smiling. "Life is a horned toad chariot race. I hadn't ever thought of it that way, but it makes some sense."

"One thing though," Charlie said. "I don't know if any of you remember, or saw it since everyone was watching their own horned toad, but one toad ran straight and true down the race course and off into the prairie."

"I never knew that," Robert Earl said. "I was watching my toad, which I had thought would be the finest racing horned toad ever harnessed to a chariot, take off the wrong direction and get stomped to death. I never looked at any of the rest of them. There was such confusion and all that I just assumed all of them met an ugly end."

"Whose horned toad actually ran the race course?" Billy Rex asked.

"Had to have been Charlie's," I said, remembering that he won everything when we were kids.

"Nope," Charlie said. "Mine started okay, but then turned back and ran straight into the stomping ground, just like he thought it over and decided he'd rather commit suicide than pull that chariot. It was Son's. It ran straight and true. I'm sure Son saw it, but he was so busy laughing at the mess the rest of us were in that he never said anything about it."

"I'll be damned," I mused.

"Imagine that," Robert Earl exclaimed.

"You know, Robert Earl," Billy Rex finally said, "if your analogy that life is a horned toad chariot race is true, that means there is hope for some of us—that some of the things we plan can actually happen."

Robert Earl thought for a moment and then answered, "I guess you're right. I focused on my own disaster and the general melee. I never noticed that there was some success."

"Is it a little spooky that the one who succeeded then is also the one who seems to have had the most satisfying life since then?" I said.

"That is a little spooky," Robert Earl added.

"Well, at least so far," Billy Rex said.

"What do you mean?" Charlie asked.

"Well, this time my horned toad—me—might have gotten stomped a few times, but I ain't dead. I'm still in the race. I plan to get to the finish line."

We all laughed, and then lapsed into silence as we sat. After a few minutes, Robert Earl asked, "What's the difference between what Son did and what we do? I mean besides the fact that we make more money sitting on our asses than he made doing hard physical labor out in all sorts of weather?"

"You mean aside from that one little minor thing?" I asked as I smiled at his description. "Well, I guess the way you measure success would be one thing," I answered after thinking a minute about his question. "In my business we measure a man's success by his title and how much money he makes. The work—what he actually does—doesn't really matter all that much. What matters is how much money he can squeeze out of it. Power is part of it too, but power is measured by money. Whether a man is really good at his job is not so important as how much money he makes from it.

"I think it's different here," I continued as I stood up, stretched, and walked to the edge of the platform to look up at the immense starry sky. "I think it is different out here," I repeated, slowly, struggling to find the right words to express how I felt. "I don't think money is the primary factor in success here. I think what matters, in the eyes of your peers, is how well you do your job. If you work hard and do your job well—are a good cowboy—you're considered a success, or at least a decent human being."

I walked back to the bench and sat down beside Robert Earl. I leaned back against the wall and said, "I think what I'm trying to say is that out here the *work* is what is important, how well you do your job, whereas in my world how well you do your job is not nearly as important as what you can *acquire* for doing that job.

"In Son's world, because the work itself was the object, his days were full of meaningful activity. In my job the work itself is more or less meaningless. All I really do all day is give people permission to do what they already know they should do. I don't really produce anything. There is no pride or satisfaction at the end of the day, except that I'm one day closer to a paycheck. In Son's world every day was an accomplishment. Every day was an exercise in what's important. That *has* to be more satisfying."

"There's a kind of code of ethics or code of conduct out here that seems to really mean something too," Robert Earl added. "There's a code of behavior they really seem to try to live by. What that means is that they have a rulebook, or guidebook, for their entire lives," Robert Earl concluded. "Damn. Wouldn't that make life a lot simpler?"

"God, wouldn't it," I sighed. "You know, I can remember thinking—as a kid—that I'd be glad when I was a grown-up because then I'd know all the answers, know what to do all the time. Now that I'm supposed to be a grown-up, I realize I still don't know squat. In fact I think I just know more reasons to be confused. I wonder if my kids think I know all of the answers, like I thought about our parents? I wonder how they'd feel if they knew I was scared to death most of the time because I don't have any damned idea what to do. That's a hell of a way to go through life isn't it? Scared!"

Charlie still had not participated in the conversation, but I noticed that he was listening intently, facing the three of us now rather than turning away.

Robert Earl got up and walked over to the nearest support post and leaned against it, looking out into the night. "I think about family a lot lately," he said, sadly. "I live a long way from any of my immediate family and none of us cousins are close anymore. I don't feel like the people I work with are any sort of extended family for me. I remember how we all used to go on those giant family camp-outs in Fort Davis and Balmorhea when we were kids. I was really happy then, and I'm pretty sure our parents were too, most of the time. What happened to us? Why aren't we a real family any more?"

"You said something a moment ago about how things hadn't turned out the way you thought they would. What did you think you were going to do when we were kids?" I asked.

"You know what I really wanted to do?" he replied. "I wanted to be a park ranger. As far back as I can remember, that's what I wanted to do. I think it came from those camp-outs we had at the park in the mountains, or the swimming expeditions at Balmorhea State Park. Maybe it was because I was happiest then, but that was what I wanted to do."

"Well, why didn't you?" I said.

"When I got out of school I applied with the Park Service, but they weren't hiring, and the Workers' Comp Commission was. I thought I'd work for one state agency till a job came open at the one I really wanted. It never happened though, and after a while I just sort of got into a routine at the commission, and it seemed too much trouble to change. Next thing I knew, twenty years had gone by.

"Things haven't been all that bad at the commission. The hours are good, benefits are good, and pay isn't awful. I'm satisfied most of the time. But you know, sometimes when I'm laying in bed waiting to go to sleep, I still picture myself in a park ranger uniform driving one of those cool park ranger trucks.

"What did you guys want to do? Have you always planned to be where you are now?" Robert Earl asked, shifting the attention away from himself.

"I'm not sure I had a plan," Billy Rex answered. "I just wanted to get out of school and get a job. I just sort of drifted into the business department and got a business degree. Then the bank offered me a job, and I'm still there. I guess I'm just a creature of habit."

"I planned to be the head coach at Notre Dame by now," I said. "I loved coaching, but when I got into the college level I really got turned off by recruiting, and when I got married I felt like it didn't pay enough to support a family, so I went back and got a degree in hospital administration. The pay has been better, but I never had as much fun as I did when I was coaching. When I'm laying there in bed at night going through the what if's of my life, I see myself on the sideline at a packed stadium."

"I planned to be living in a mansion in Beverly Hills by now," Charlie suddenly spoke up, surprising us. He stood up and walked to the other side of the platform as he spoke. "I was never sure if I would be an actor or a singer, but I was sure I would be successful in some way in the entertainment business…and be richer than Midas. But now," he added, "I just wish I'd gotten a teaching degree." He stared at the stars. "I'd love to get a job teaching at some small school—somewhere like Alpine, or Marfa, or Fort Davis even. Maybe coach a little. Settle down in one spot." His voice sort of trailed off as he finished his thought.

"Well, why don't you go back to school and get it?" Billy Rex asked.

"Yeah. Why not?" I said. "If that's what you'd really like to do."

"Naah. Y'all don't understand. I was an athlete when I went to college. I wasn't into actual class work. I played football and baseball for four years, and I probably have less than two years of actual credits, and most of them don't actually relate to one another. It'd take me three or four years of full-time college to do that." Charlie said sadly, and then—looking up and seeming surprised to see the three of us looking intently at him—immediately changed his mood and cheerfully added, "And besides, I'm too damned good looking to go to college now. I'd drive all them eighteen-year-old coeds wild. I still wouldn't get any real school work done."

We silently watched fireflies flame out, and looked at the millions of stars visible over A Mountain, each of us with his own thoughts.

"Damn! We're a hell of a bunch!" I exclaimed, attempting to break the melancholy mood. "Most people would think we've got the world by the balls. We got a banker, a high-ranking government bureaucrat, a hospital CEO, and a genuine celebrity and folk hero here, and all we've done is cry in our beer."

Robert Earl grinned and walked back over to sit beside me. Charlie chuckled and clapped Billy Rex on the back as he sat back down on the bench beside him.

I continued energetically, "We come home to Alpine and fall apart talking about how much better they've got it here than we do. What the hell is going on? Is Alpine, Texas, some sort of a West Texas version of Brigadoon? Have we stumbled into the twilight zone or something?"

My outburst brought chuckles from the other three.

"Brigapine," Billy Rex suggested, grinning.

"Or Alpidoon," Charlie countered, and we relaxed and sat at ease, enjoying the moment, and the beauty of the evening, the uncomfortable frankness and emotional honesty of a few minutes before behind us.

"There is one more thing I want to tell you guys," Robert Earl said slowly. He seemed to be struggling with what he wanted to say. He started to speak, opened his mouth, and then stopped. Finally he said softly, "This day and tonight have been wonderful gifts. It's made me feel like I actually had a family again, and I like that feeling. Mom and Dad both being dead means I really have no immediate family, and there's no one I'm close to. It's not a real good feeling to get old and realize you are all alone. Don't let that happen to you guys."

We sat quietly for several minutes, each of us in his own world of thought.

"Listen!" Charlie said suddenly, turning his head to look down the tracks to his right. "I think a train's coming."

We all turned our heads in that direction and listened carefully. We heard the sound of a train approaching from the west. The whistle wailed, and from the volume I judged it to be less than half a mile away. Within minutes the train roared into and through the station, streaking past us. The train passed less than fifteen feet from where we sat. We felt the vibrations the huge vehicle created as it shook and compressed the tracks, and the rapid movement of air pushed away in all directions as the engine impacted the atmosphere in front of it. The noise was deafening. For no good reason at all Charlie, then Robert Earl, and then Billy Rex and I stood and started to yell loudly back at the train in an almost angry challenge. We clenched our fists, leaned toward the train, and yelled as loudly as we could, no words, just angry noise, but the noise from the train was so loud we could not even hear ourselves, much less the others.

It was an Amtrack passenger train and—though it was well after midnight—lights glowed in the passenger cars and we could see people sitting or sleeping in the seats, although the train was moving too fast for us to make out any of the passengers' features.

On a totally stupid and beautiful impulse, I began moving closer to the tracks and unbuckling my belt. Turning my back to the train, I pulled my pants down, leaned forward at the waist, and mooned the train. I had no idea where the idea to do this had come from, but I noticed Charlie was suddenly beside me also dropping his pants, and Billy Rex and Robert Earl quickly joined suit. There we stood, four fifty-something males with our pants down, on a depot platform in West Texas, mooning the train and any passengers who might still be awake and happen to glance out. All of a sudden I felt great again. It was exhilarating!

Then the train was gone, racing away toward San Antonio or Austin. We stopped yelling and listened to it disappear into the night. We heard the whistle become more and more distant. As we pulled our pants up, almost as one person, we began to laugh uproariously. We stumbled back to the benches and sat back down limply, still laughing, giggling, and savoring the sensation of being so close to and challenging such power and force, and of doing something so absolutely foolish and inappropriate. God it was great!

"Damn that was fun!" Robert Earl finally regained enough composure to say, grinning from ear to ear. "What in the world possessed you to pull your pants down like that?"

"I don't have the slightest idea," I answered honestly as I leaned limply against the wall. "For some reason it just seemed the thing to do. I haven't done anything that stupid in years. Why did you do it with me?"

"I haven't got any idea either," he replied, still giggling. "Once you did it though I wasn't about to be left out!"

"Me neither," Billy Rex said as he struggled to catch his breath. "I wasn't about to let you have all the fun by being the only dumbass here!"

"Can you imagine," Charlie asked, "what anyone who happened to look out the window would have thought? Four shriveled old white asses looking them in the eye!"

That started another round of laughing. Charlie imitated someone just happening to turn his head to look out the window, turning away, then snapping his head back in a double take to see if what he thought he had seen was still there. Since the sight would have been gone by then, he pretended to look confused and then shook his head as if to say he could not have seen what he thought he saw. It was great. It took us several minutes to calm down, to stop laughing.

"Speak for yourself on that shriveled part," I said between laughs. "My ass still looks pretty damn good!"

"Yeah, the shriveled part is on the other side with you isn't it?" Charlie retorted. "Every since Granny made a pass at you this afternoon!"

That started another round of exhausting hysterical laughter. Several minutes passed before each of us was able to regain composure and sit back against the wall, resting, and reflecting.

At last I broke the spell of the moment. "I hate to be a spoilsport, but this bunch of old farts better get their old heinies to bed or none of us is going to make the meeting with Starlene in the morning."

"Yeah, you're right," Billy Rex said sadly, not making any move to get up.

"Unfortunate but true," Robert Earl mused.

"It's hell to get old," Charlie added as he took the lead and got up from the bench.

The four of us stood up and walked slowly through the starry night, across Holland Avenue to the hotel. Cousins, friends, and family again.

Chapter 24

Having slept little, when my Sunday morning wakeup call startled
me awake I felt as if I had not been to bed at all. After grudgingly arising,
showering, shaving, and packing, I trudged down the stairs, still half asleep,
in the same trousers I had worn the previous evening, a hunter green knit
golf shirt, and cross-trainer athletic shoes. I stopped on the second floor to
pay my bill, and then went downstairs to the restaurant. We had agreed to
meet for breakfast, and then follow Charlie to Son's house for the meeting
with Starlene. Billy Rex, Robert Earl, and Charlie were already sitting at a
table in the middle of the room. Charlie wore jeans and athletic shoes and
a blue with yellow striped rugby shirt. Billy Rex also had on a pair of jeans
and a short-sleeved yellow cotton shirt. Robert Earl wore what appeared to
be the same trousers he had worn last night, a pair of deck shoes with no
socks, and a pullover maroon sweater. There was also a fourth man sitting
at the table with them. He wore what appeared to be some sort of uniform,
but it did not register with me immediately. Only two other tables were
occupied, one by what appeared to be a couple of real estate agents, the other
by two cowboys in jeans and work shirts, their hats on the empty chairs at
their table.

The restaurant that used to be the hotel lobby was large—perhaps sixty
feet deep and forty across. The floor was Mexican tile of all different sizes.
Large arched windows opened out into what had been a courtyard during
the hotel's prime, but now appeared to be a flower garden. Bright sunlight
broadcasted through the windows. Colorful Mexican tile covered the lower
portion of the walls, contrasting with white plaster the rest of the way to the
ceiling. A huge fireplace with an ornate wooden mantel dominated the rear
of the room. Several leather-looking sofas were arranged to face the fireplace.
Between the fireplace and the front where I stood were tables of various sizes,
all covered with white tablecloths. Baskets hung throughout the room, with
erupting plants and ferns. There was an eclectic mix of Indian, Mexican, and
modern art on the walls. The decor did not match either the predominant
western culture of Alpine or the historic nature of the hotel, but it was a
pleasing overall effect.

Making my way to the table occupied by my cousins and the unknown
man, I dropped my bag beside one of the two empty chairs, and sat down
heavily. A large pot of coffee was on the table, and I filled the cup in front of

me. It was not until after I had taken a long, eye-opening drink that I finally looked at my cousins. I hoped my eyes did not look as bad as theirs. It was then that I finally noticed the badge on the stranger, and the gun strapped to his hip.

"We have a problem, Tom," Charlie said. "Someone dug up Son's grave last night."

"What?" was all I could think to say. What he had said just did not register.

The uniformed man stuck his hand across the table to me, saying, "Mike Cooter. I'm a deputy sheriff here in Brewster County. I tracked you guys down through Vernon and Starlene and came over to give you the news."

"Come again," I said, confused. "What happened?"

"Well, the simple version of it," Mike Cooter explained, "is that someone dug up Son's grave last night."

"Dug up his grave," I repeated dully. "Did they steal his body or something?"

"No," Mike Cooter continued. "As near as we can tell they just dug him up, opened the coffin, and sat him up in it. We can't tell that anything was done to the body at all."

"Why would anyone do that?" I asked, still not fully understanding what had happened.

Even though he had likely gone through the same conversation with the others, the deputy patiently explained to me that they had no idea yet. "We were hoping you fellows might have some ideas. I actually came to ask if you would come over to the cemetery with me to look around—see if anything rings any bells. Vernon and Star are already there."

"Sure," I said. "Do you mind if I have a quick cup of coffee and a doughnut or something to settle my stomach first?"

"Certainly," the deputy said. "How about if I go on over there, and you guys meet me there when you finish?"

All of us voiced our agreement, and the deputy rose and left the restaurant. I looked around at my cousins. They all looked stunned, in addition to being hung over.

"Anyone got any idea what this is all about?" I asked, mainly in Charlie's direction.

"I really don't have any idea," Charlie said. "My first thought was that some of the guys at the wake last night got too drunk and decided to have one last drink with Son. That's the only idea I can come up with."

"That would make sense," Billy Rex said. "But don't you think they would have put him back afterward?"

"Hell if I know," Charlie said. "I never had a drink with a dead person. I don't know what the protocol is."

Downing a quick cup of coffee, I asked the waitress to bring me a couple of doughnuts and a cup of coffee to go. She brought it back to the table along with to-go coffee cups for the other three cousins. We all contributed to a pile of money on the table, grabbed our bags, and headed for the cemetery again.

It only took a few minutes to drive to the cemetery, unlike yesterday's slow drive behind the funeral wagon. We drove through the gate and stopped a row over from Son's grave. Vernon, Starlene, and Roy Don were there, standing with Mike Cooter and several other men in sheriff's department garb or police uniforms. Yellow crime scene tape had been stretched around the grave and tied to bushes, trees, and even tall monuments. As I approached the scene, I could see that the grave had indeed been dug up. A pile of fresh dirt was next to the open mouth of the grave we had seen Son's coffin go into yesterday. I ducked under the yellow boundary tape and approached the grave.

As I walked to the side of the opened grave I looked into it. Son was propped up at the end of the coffin, like he had decided to sit up and look around. His legs were extended straight in front of him, the toes of his boots pointing up at the open sky. His arms were hanging by his side and his hands lying in his lap. His eyes were still closed, but his head was looking straight toward the other end of the grave. The coffin itself was empty except for some dirt that had obviously fallen from the edge of the hole into it.

"Damn!" I exclaimed. I didn't know what else to say. "Damn!"

"You can say that again," Robert Earl added as he stood beside me.

"Damn!" I said.

"Will you look at that?" Billy Rex said as he joined us.

Charlie walked to Starlene and they embraced silently.

"And we don't have any idea why someone would do something like that?" I asked in the direction of the uniforms.

One, who I recognized as Sheriff Bill Davis, said, "Not one damned idea. It's the damndest thing any of us have ever seen. We were hoping one of you could remember something that might give us a place to start."

"Well I've run into a lot of people since I been here, but no one said anything like, 'Let's go dig up Son,'" I said. "Was anything weird done to him?"

"Near as we can tell, nothing was done," said the funeral director, who also acted as the medical examiner in Alpine. "There's not a mark on him, and nothing is missing. He does not appear to have been abused in any way, other than being set up. Looking at what was done, or not done, all I can say is it looked like someone just wanted to see him one more time."

"Damn!" I said again. "That's just weird."

"Well what do we do now?" Charlie asked.

"Well," said the sheriff, taking off his hat and running his hand through thinning hair, "this is my first case like this. Digging up a grave is a crime, for sure. But there appears to have been no grave robbing or desecration of the corpse. I'd say we search the scene with a fine tooth comb, photograph everything, and get him back in the grave. That will take most of the day. Why don't we plan on reburying him in the morning? Does the family have any objection, or want another ceremony?"

Charlie and Starlene talked for a minute, and then Starlene and Vernon excused themsleves and left, saying they would see us at Son's place.

Charlie said, "Let's just get the preacher to come over and say a prayer and do it. We don't want to make a big deal of it."

"I'll contact the minister and make the arrangements," the funeral director said. "I'll call Starlene to let you know what time is convenient."

"Just one thing," I suggested. "When you are ready to bury him again, don't get gravediggers to do it. How about letting us do it?" I indicated the four cousins standing around the hole.

"There's probably some statute that forbids family members burying their own," the director mused. "But I'd put you on the books as my employees if it's okay with the sheriff." With that he looked questioningly at the sheriff.

"I reckon if I grab a shovel and pitch in too it will be just fine," Sheriff Davis said. After some more discussion with the sheriff and undertaker, the only thing we agreed on was that none of us had any idea what had happened.

Charlie motioned the four cousins to join him off to the side. "We need to go out to Son's house now," she whispered. "I'm not sure how, but it probably has something to do with this."

"Should we tell the sheriff or the police?" Billy Rex asked.

"No. Starlene says we'll understand after we talk."

As I turned to leave, I noticed that Robert Earl was looking intently into the open grave at Son. I walked over and stood beside him.

"Look at his face," Robert Earl whispered. "Is it possible that he's smiling?"

I looked at Son. There did seem to be just the trace of a smile. "Surely not," I denied. "It's probably just a grimace. You know, as the skin tightens."

"Yeah. Maybe," Robert Earl said. "But it sure looks like a smile to me. Spooky!"

I looked back at Son. It *did* look like a smile, and it *was* spooky. Robert Earl and I hurried to our vehicles for the trip out of the cemetery.

Chapter 25

Before I got to my truck, the pager on my belt erupted in shrill repetitive beeps. Looking at the tiny screen, I saw that the call originated from Robert Blake's home number in Austin. I toyed with the idea of ignoring the call, but curiosity and habit were too strong. I dialed Blake's home number on my cell phone as we all pulled out from the cemetery in a caravan. Charlie led, Billy Rex next, then Robert Earl, and I brought up the rear.

Blake answered the telephone before the first ring had finished. "Tom? Is that you?"

"Yes, it's me Robert," I answered. "What's up?"

"Tom, we *really* need you to get back here. This situation is getting out of hand. Dr. Kerley has joined Dr. Howard and Dr. Fine. I think they agreed to support his new imaging machine if he'd back them at the board meeting. You need to get back here and stop this before it goes any further."

Something was not ringing true as I listened to the nearly panicked Blake. My returning to Austin and solving the problem should have been the last thing he would want. My absence had given him the opportunity to make a move on my job. Something was not right. Then I had a flash of logical assumption.

"The doctors told you they wouldn't support you as my replacement, didn't they Robert?" I said.

No sound came from the cell phone for perhaps thirty seconds. Then Blake said, with defeat in his voice, "They said they would only support a physician as the next CEO of the hospital. They said they had had enough incompetent administration by non-professionals."

I could not resist snorting a gleefully derisive laugh. "Damn Robert!" I said. "It sounds like you've nailed your own ass to the wall." I could not help but enjoy the position he found himself in.

"Tom, we can talk about that later," Blake said, making no attempt to conceal his desperation. "We can put a stop to all this if you will just get back here and open negotiations with these doctors. Paul Jordan is going to meet me at the hospital in about an hour to plot strategy. We can call you on your cell phone and make plans while you drive back."

"I don't know, Robert," I replied. "I've still got some things to do here. I'm not sure when I'm coming back. Hell!" I suddenly said, "I'm not even sure if I'm coming back."

"Now don't talk like that!" Blake pleaded, sounding as if he was near a total nervous breakdown. "I'll call you when Paul gets here."

"I don't know Robert," I said. "I'll think about it." I pushed the button ending the call. I turned my attention to following Charlie. Ordinarily a situation such as the one that had evolved at the hospital would have commanded my full attention, but the events of the last couple of days in Alpine made it seem almost inconsequential. It took me only a few blocks to put it out of my mind.

We drove westward out of Alpine. Charlie led in a green Ford Explorer that appeared to be new. Billy Rex was in a four-year-old gold Chevrolet Suburban, and Robert Earl drove behind him in a white Toyota Celica that looked to be at least ten years old. I brought up the rear in my truck.

It was a bright, clear, sunny day. There was a brisk October coolness in the mountain air. We headed toward Twin Peaks, massive against the western sky. We passed the Cable house at the western edge of town and kept going until we were about five miles west of town, climbing steadily if not steeply toward the mountains.

I noticed the left turn signal blinking on Charlie's Explorer. He turned off the road and stopped at a gate in the fence. Billy Rex, Robert Earl, and I pulled off behind him. There was just enough room for all of us to line up at the gate with my truck barely off the highway. Charlie got out to open the gate, left it open, climbed back into his vehicle, and drove through. Billy Rex and Robert Earl drove through behind him. After following my three cousins into the pasture beyond the gate, I stopped, got out, and walked back to the gate. I swung it shut and hitched the chain catch over the post.

I climbed back into my truck and started out after the other three, following a dirt road across open land southward, low across the face of the Twin Peaks. The terrain was gently sloping grassland broken only by a few sotol stalks sticking up at irregular intervals. The slope was so gentle that the road simply sloped with the contour. My truck tilted downhill to the left as I drove.

After we had traveled about three miles, the dirt road curved to the right and, after a small rise, came into a mostly level section on the side of the mountain, about five hundred yards across. In the center of this area was a house, a windmill with a tank, and a small pole barn. Livestock corrals extended out from one side of the small barn. Vernon's truck and Roy Don's Volvo station wagon were parked by the house. Charlie pulled up beside the Volvo, and Billy Rex, Robert Earl, and I pulled up and parked behind the first three vehicles. We got out of our vehicles and walked toward the front of the house. I studied the place as I walked.

The house was wood frame on a rock and concrete foundation, painted white with green trim. It was square, two windows to a side. A door separated the windows in the back. Three rock and concrete steps led up to the uncovered back door. In the front, a porch as wide as the house extended out about ten feet. The roof over the porch was supported by four rough-hewn log beams. Three Adirondack-style wooden chairs waited on the porch. I imagined that with both doors open, as well as many of the screened windows, even a light breeze would cool the house nicely. The town of Alpine stretched out in the valley below us to the east, and Twin Peaks loomed above us to the west.

The windmill stood about thirty yards in front of the porch, a round rock and concrete water tank next to it, the rocks reddish brown against the dull gray of the concrete. The top of the tank was five feet above ground, and it was a good fifteen feet across. On the one side of the tank were concrete steps from the ground to the rim, providing access to the tank. I experienced a brief flash of a memory of kids swimming naked in such tanks many summers ago. Next to the larger tank was a smaller stock watering trough about two feet high. An overflow pipe from the top of the large tank was the water source for the smaller tank. The windmill was made of wood, sturdy six-inch by six-inch beams that had weathered gray. The metal fan blades on the top of the tower were turning lazily in an almost indiscernible breeze. The iron sucker rod in the middle of the tower was moving very slowly up and down, pumping a thin stream of water that trickled from a pipe extending from the windmill to the large tank. I could hear the creak of the metal blades as they turned slowly, and the splash of the water entering the tank.

The barn and small corral were a little farther, perhaps fifty yards from the house. The barn was the pole barn variety—long, thick poles set directly into the ground, roof beams laid across the tops, and three sides and the roof covered with tin. Animals could enter the barn on the open side, to the east, to avoid the cold winds and rains that usually blew in from the north and northwest. Wooden posts set into the ground supported the fence of rough-hewn planks. A wooden gate interrupted the fence on the eastern side, toward the water tank.

A solitary black horse stood in the corral. The animal appeared well-fed and well-groomed. It stood at the fence with its head extended over the fence, intently watching as we approached the house. The animal was motionless except for an occasional tail flick to shoo flies.

Billy Rex, Robert Earl, and I followed Charlie around to the front of the house and up the steps onto the front porch. We paused there to study the view. To our left, the town of Alpine spread down Alpine Valley toward SR Mountain in the distance. The red brick buildings of Sul Ross University were clearly visible on the side of the far mountain, above the rest of the town. The dome of the Baptist Church could also be seen near the middle of the town. To the right of town was A Mountain, and to the right of A Mountain, directly outward from the front of the porch, was another valley, very similar to Alpine Valley except that there was no sign of human habitation. This valley was about five miles across at the far, narrower end, and appeared to widen to almost ten miles in the center. Blue mountains in the distance closed and bordered the valley. The wide valley floor was grassland, and a few cattle grazed in the distance. To the right side of the porch, Twin Peaks loomed above us, a grassy slope rising from the small level area and transitioning to rugged and rocky terrain only a few hundred feet above the level of the house. It was a spectacularly beautiful scene. It was hard to turn away, but Charlie finally moved toward the door. The rest of us followed, looking back.

The screen door snapped shut behind us as we entered into a large living room. The room was furnished with a sofa that appeared to be covered with cowhides, and a large lounge chair covered with the same material. A coffee table made of a large slab of polished stone sitting on four mesquite stumps sat in front of the sofa, and a table-model television sat on a wooden box in a corner. Bookshelves had been built into the wall from the floor up about three feet. The shelves were packed with books and magazines of all descriptions. A small reading lamp sat on another wooden box next to the lounge chair. The floor was of well-worn pine. The walls were also natural pine.

To the left, the house was open. The rear area was the kitchen, separated from a dining area by a waist-high counter. In the dining area between the kitchen and the living room, a rustic wooden table about six feet long and four feet wide exhibited the marks of many years' use. Around the table were straight-backed wooden chairs with cowhide seats. A small fire burned warmly against the October morning chill in a rock fireplace near the table. With the wood floors and the natural pine walls, the interior of the house resembled what one might expect in a hunting cabin—not luxurious, but utilitarian and quite comfortable.

Star, Vernon, and Roy Don were sitting at the table. The three of them were drinking coffee from a pot steaming on the stove. Robert Earl went immediately to the kitchen, found a coffee cup, and filled it. He joined the others at the table. Billy Rex and I followed. Vernon got up and put another piece of wood on the fire.

"Man! That's one hell of a view off the front porch!" Robert Earl said.

"Isn't it beautiful?" Starlene agreed. "Son, Vernon, and I have sat there for hours just talking and looking at the country."

"Spectacular!" I added. "I don't think I was even aware that valley behind A Mountain was there. It's prettier than Alpine Valley, I think."

"Son used to call it Peaceful Valley," Starlene said. "He used to say that if he were having a bad day he could sit on the porch and imagine himself riding out there in Peaceful Valley, and the cares of the world just went away."

"I can sure understand that," I said, with envy, as I looked back over my shoulder out the front windows.

"How did Son afford this place Star?" Billy Rex asked. "This is a nice place for someone who worked for cowboy wages."

"Well," Star said, as she took another drink of her coffee, "the place is actually pretty small, only about ten acres around this clearing where the house is. Everything else you see is owned by the big ranchers in the area, and Son leased grazing rights from them. Those cattle you see in the valley are actually his, although the land is not. Was not," she corrected herself.

"He bought this place from a rancher who owns the land to the north of here. The deed gives him rights to an unpaved road across the main ranch. That's the road you all came in on.

"He actually bought it about twenty years ago, and didn't get it paid off until about a year ago. He built this house mostly by himself. Vernon and I helped him, and so did a lot of his friends. He'd just build a little more when he had the money. It's been twenty years of off and on building to get it to what there is now."

"That's amazing," Billy Rex said, shaking his head. "Most of the people I deal with make ten times what Son must have made, and still manage to wind up with nothing. Son is frugal enough to wind up owning this great place. That's a hell of an accomplishment."

"I'm sure as hell impressed," Robert Earl added.

"Well Son didn't need much, and didn't spend much money on himself." Starlene continued, "So he put everything he made into this place. This place was his life."

"And you guys need to understand," Vernon said. "Our dreams and aspirations are not as large or as fast moving as you might be used to in the big city. Our dreams move slowly and gratifications come more slowly out here."

"There's a song about that, isn't there?" I asked, trying to remember. "A Willie Nelson song, I think."

"Hey, I know that song," Charlie said. "I'll sing it for you later."

"Do you guys remember," I said slowly, thinking back to our youth, "when we used to save soda bottles to get money for the movies? Remember that Son was in charge of our bank? And remember that he would never let us spend any of our movie money for candy or anything else but movies? He wouldn't let us get off track. I guess he did the same thing to pay for this place."

"I'd forgotten about that," Charlie smiled as he remembered. "He'd squeeze a nickel till the buffalo crapped in his hand even back then," and the rest of us laughed, also remembering.

"How come Son never got married and had a family?" I asked.

"Well it sure as hell wasn't because he didn't have a chance," Vernon replied with a grin. "I don't know if you noticed, but at the funeral it looked like every other person was an unaccompanied female. Son cut quite a swath through the single female population in Alpine. Every single girl and widow in Alpine loved him, but he just wasn't interested in getting married."

"Early on I think that was because he wanted to put all his energy into getting this place," Starlene explained. "But after he found out about his heart, he said he didn't want to leave a widow and kids with no real means of support."

"Damn. That's depressing!" Robert Earl said.

"No. No," Starlene replied. "Son was happy. He loved this place, and his stock, and being a cowboy, more than anything else in the world. And he had a lot of friends, and he had his family. Vernon and I were here, and he kept up with all of you more than you probably knew."

There was a lull in the conversation so I took the opportunity to say, "Star, you said at the cemetery that what you wanted to talk about might have something to do with Son being dug up last night. I'm at a loss as to why someone would have done that, so tell us what is going on."

"It has to do with this," she answered after a pregnant pause, and she pointed toward a legal-sized manila envelope lying on the table in front of her. I had not noticed it until she directed our attention to it.

"About a year ago, Son gave me this envelope," Starlene continued as she took several sheets of paper from the envelope. "It was sealed, and he asked me to open it and read it only after he died."

"That must have been tough," I said. "Were you able to resist?"

"Yes. I locked it in a little safe Vernon and I have at the house, and pretty much forgot about it. Then, this week, when we read Son's will, there were instructions for me to read the letter and then share it with any other family members I thought appropriate. I remembered it then and got it out of the safe. I read it this weekend."

She hesitated for a moment as if regrouping her thoughts.

"Well?" Robert Earl asked. "Tell us what's in it. I can't stand the suspense much longer."

"Rather than try to tell you about it, I'm just going to read it," Starlene answered. "I wanted to do it out here so we could have privacy. You'll understand after I get through."

She took several sheets of paper from the envelope, unfolded them, and began to read.

"Dear Star, and anyone else reading or listening, I've kept this story to myself for a lot of years, and I thought about taking it to the grave with me, but I decided it was something family had a right to know."

I felt a cold shiver as I realized that Son was talking to us from his grave again.

"One night in September of 1961—I remember when because it was right after Granddad died. We had all gone to the funeral that day, and several relatives had come over and were staying the night. After supper I went out and climbed up in the cottonwood tree in the front yard to have a little privacy. I did that sometimes to get away."

"I remember Son climbing up in trees and sitting on a branch for hours like that," Roy Don said. "He started doing it when we were too little to follow him. He got away from the smaller kids."

Starlene started reading again.

"After I had been up there for a while, Daddy, Momma, Uncle Tom, and Uncle Ray all came outside. They sat and talked on the porch for a while. Then they

dragged those old metal chairs we had on the porch over under the tree I was sitting in. I figured they wanted more privacy. I thought about saying something, but then I realized that both Momma and Uncle Tom were crying. Then I was afraid to say anything. I'd never seen Uncle Tom, or any grown man, cry. I was high enough up in the limbs, and it was night, that they couldn't see me, so I just sat real still and listened.

"After a little while I figured out that they were talking about when they had been in foster homes when Granddad had to go off to work, during the Depression. That was the first time I heard that Momma had been assaulted. I didn't exactly understand what that meant at that age, but I got the idea that Momma had been hurt in some way. We've all heard some of that story from relatives since then. It was when they were on the Clinton farm up by Seymour. I heard the whole story that night, and it was pretty awful.

"The Clintons had two boys who were about eighteen. Momma was sixteen. Uncle Ray was fourteen, and Uncle Tom was twelve. The first time those two brothers assaulted her, Momma told the Clintons about it. Their reaction was to call her a liar and whip her, and just to make a point they whipped Ray and Tom too. And this was not just a belt whipping, they whipped them with a piece of rawhide rope across their backs and legs until they could not stand up. That's how they knew when to stop—when they collapsed. Momma said she tried to tell Granddad when he came for a visit, but he wouldn't believe her either."

Starlene stopped for a moment. She took a handkerchief from Vernon and wiped her eyes. I had a lump in my throat that felt like a basketball, and I could see that everyone else at the table was similarly affected. I heard Charlie muttering, "Goddamn bastards!"

"Momma said that night that the main reason she finally stopped fighting was that she was afraid that they were going to kill Tom. He was just a skinny little kid who couldn't fight back. After it had been going on for a while, the two brothers started tying Tom and Ray to the fence in the barn stall, and making them watch while the two of them had at her. If they said anything, the Clinton brothers would beat the crap out of them while they were tied up. Momma told them to keep quiet.

"This went on for over a year. The three of them tried to run away several times, but they always got caught, brought back, and beat worse. Once they even rode a cow for several miles to keep from making tracks the Clintons could follow, but they still got caught. Finally, Momma convinced Ray and Tom to run away

without her, thinking they'd have a better chance with just the two of them, and that the Clinton brothers didn't care too much about finding Ray and Tom. They just wanted to keep Momma around.

"Uncle Tom and Uncle Ray both cried like babies that night when I was up in the tree. Tom said that leaving Momma there was the worst thing he had ever done in his life, and it had haunted him every day of his life since. Uncle Ray said pretty much the same thing, but Momma said that if they hadn't gone when they did, one or both of them would be dead now. She said the Clinton boys would have beaten them to death just for fun, and she could not bear the thought of that.

"Anyway, Ray and Tom got away when Uncle Ray was fifteen and Uncle Tom was thirteen. They hopped a freight train just outside Seymour and rode it all the way to West Texas. They got lucky and got a job on a ranch there. Soon after that, Granddad got married again, and came and got Momma and took her home. She said the Clinton boys told her that if she ever told anyone what had happened they would come find her and kill her and her brothers. Momma never tried to tell Granddad about it after she came home. Ray and Tom came home for visits, and wanted to tell Granddad, but Momma wouldn't let them. She wanted to let the past die. She said she was ashamed, and did not want to bring it on the rest of the family. So only Momma, Ray, and Tom knew. She must have told Daddy sometime later, because he seemed to know about it that night. Sometime, years later, she told enough to her sisters for the family to put most of it together.

"That night they decided that since Granddad was dead, and because it had been eating on them for so long, it was time to do something about it. I did not understand what that meant, and they were not specific about any plan, but the last thing they did that night was to swear to each other to keep this a secret, to tell no one about what had happened, or whatever they did about it. I stayed up in that tree for a long time after they left. Then I came down and snuck in to bed, and I've never told anyone about that night until now. And that is only the first part of the story.

"About a month later in November, in deer season, Daddy said that he and Uncle Tom and Uncle Ray were going to go hunting for a weekend. Usually I got to go, but this time they said I couldn't go. I was pretty hurt by that and spent some time spying on them for spite. What I saw was Daddy filling every gas can he could find and putting them in the trunk of his old Chevy. He must have put fifty gallons of gas in there. They loaded their bedrolls and their rifles into the back too. They said they were going down in Big Bend Park poaching, and would be back Sunday night. For some reason though, I knew that was not what they were going to do. I sensed that whatever they were going to do had to do with what I

had heard them talk about that night.

"I'm still not sure why, but the next morning I got up before anyone and was waiting when they got to the car. The sun had not even started to come up yet. It was still pitch dark and cold.

"Daddy asked what I was doing up and out there. He said he'd told me already I couldn't go with them.

"'I know you're not going hunting,' I told them. Then I told them how I had heard everything they had talked about the night Granddad was buried, that I figured that what they were going to do had something to do with that, and that I was going with them.

"That shocked them. I was scared to death. I was so scared I was shaking like I had cold shivers. But I had taken a stand, and I was not going to back down—no matter what.

"The three of them went around to the other side of the car and talked among themselves for awhile. Then they went to the car and Daddy said to get in—that he guessed I was enough of a man now to take part in man things, and since I knew why they were going, I deserved to go.

"I went with them. When we got back Daddy asked me to swear that I would not tell anyone about what had happened on the trip until after he and Momma were dead.

"I swore, and he said, 'After we are all gone, you can decide if you want to tell your brothers or not, and any of Tom and Ray's kids.' I've thought about telling you many times, but I swore I wouldn't tell. So I've kept this to myself all these years. Now I'm going to tell it to you, and you can decide among yourselves if you tell anyone else afterward. I'm sorry it worked out that I had to tell it to you in a letter, but that can't be helped now. I'll try to tell everything I can remember."

Chapter 26

We listened intently as Star continued reading the incredible story in Son's words.

"Daddy drove most of the morning that day. I sat up front with him, but we didn't talk much. Daddy was mad at me and I was afraid to ask any questions, so I just sat and watched the country go by. It was cold and windy, and most of the plants were bare, so there was not much to look at. The farther we got from Alpine the flatter the country got. It would have been depressing even if I wasn't already scared.

"That afternoon Uncle Tom and Uncle Ray took turns driving while Daddy and I got in the back and tried to sleep some, but I was too nervous to sleep. Uncle Tom and Uncle Ray took turns driving and argued about who got to drive and how long. Thinking back on it now I believe they were full of fear and nervous energy and relieved to have something to do.

"After a while I figured out we were headed for Seymour from listening to the talk. We were going to the farm where they had been abused as foster kids. It's about four hundred miles from Alpine to Seymour as the crow flies, but we didn't go a direct route. First we drove up into New Mexico, to Hobbs, and then turned east and came back into Texas in the Panhandle. We kept zigging and zagging north and south and I'm guessing we actually drove almost six hundred miles. I learned that on the return trip we were going to leave Seymour heading east for what Uncle Tom called 'a ways,' and then 'drift south' close to the Mexico border before turning back west toward Alpine. I heard Uncle Tom tell Uncle Ray that if anyone ever remembered seeing us, they hoped our direction would confuse people as to where we came from. We stopped at remote roadside parks and side roads to eat the food we had brought and to refill the gas tank from the cans of gas in the trunk. As I look back on it now, I think it was a pretty good plan. It was a common old car driven by three men and a boy who really did not stand out in any way. We never stopped at a restaurant or filling station, never talked to anyone, and hoped no one took notice of us or remembered us. From all the effort at not being noticed it did not take me long to guess that we were not going back for a social visit, and the more I thought about what we might be going for, the more scared I got.

"It was after dark on Saturday night when we arrived in Seymour. Uncle Tom and Uncle Ray remembered the way to the farm well enough to drive right to it without asking directions or losing time searching. Uncle Ray was driving

when we found the turn off the main road. He turned onto a dirt road and stopped after going a hundred yards or so and turned off the car's headlights.

"I asked why we were stopping and Uncle Ray told me he wanted to let his eyes get adjusted to the dark. He wanted to drive the rest of the way without lights so no one would see us coming. I remember sitting there in that car in the dark with the only sound coming from the engine running. No one said anything. I was so scared by now I was about to mess my pants.

"While we were sitting there Daddy said to me that he wanted me to just do what he told me and be quiet, that I wasn't to talk again till we left this place. He asked me if I understood, and I said that I did.

"Finally Uncle Tom said that he could see pretty good and Uncle Ray agreed that he thought he could see well enough to keep the car on the road. That's when Uncle Tom sort of sighed and said, 'Well, let's get this over with.' I remember actually shivering when he said that.

"Uncle Ray slowly drove the car down the dirt road. He cussed under his breath a couple of times when the wheels hit ruts he couldn't see and the car jerked to one side, but he kept it on the road and, after a mile or so, we could see a white house and a larger white barn standing out in the darkness.

"I remember Uncle Ray saying, 'This is it. This is the sorry assed damn place.' He said it in a very angry voice. Up to now everyone had been calm and talked low, but now he was mad.

"Daddy asked if they were sure this was it, and Uncle Ray said, 'This is it all right. I'll never get the sight of that barn out of my mind.' And he was still talking very mad-like. It was about then that I was sure this was going to be a very bad thing we were going to get involved in, and I was scared for Daddy more than anything else.

"We drove real slow up to the front of the house, stopped, and turned off the engine. We could see that a light was on in the back part of the house. There were no other lights on. Daddy, Uncle Ray, and Uncle Tom got out of the car. Daddy told me to move to the driver's seat and wait for them—to be prepared to drive if they needed to leave in a hurry.

"Daddy opened the trunk, and Uncle Tom reached inside and pulled out two Winchesters. He kept one and handed the other to Uncle Ray. They walked real quiet-like up onto the porch of the house. Daddy started to knock, but I saw Uncle Tom reach out and grab his arm to stop him. Uncle Tom reached up and unscrewed the bulb from the porch light. I guessed that he did not want anyone to be able to see them. When he had unscrewed the bulb he tossed it into the bushes in front of the house. Then Daddy knocked real hard on the door. At first nothing happened so

he beat on it loudly again. This time someone approached the door inside the house. The light inside the door came on, but the porch stayed dark.

"I could see that an old man opened the door. He looked to be some years older than Daddy, Uncle Tom, or Uncle Ray. He had white hair, and reading glasses pushed down low on his nose. I remember he had on denim bib overalls and a plaid shirt. He was just an average looking old man.

"He tried to see who was on the porch, but without the porch light he couldn't see. I could hear him asking, 'Who's there? What do you want?'

"And then I saw Uncle Ray move around Daddy and shove the barrel of the Winchester into the old man's chest so hard it almost knocked him down.

"I could hear Uncle Ray saying, 'You'll find out soon enough what we want you old bastard,' and each time he said something he sort of punched the guy in the chest with the gun barrel.

"Uncle Tom asked, 'Where's your brother?' and the old man said he was in the kitchen.

"I remember Uncle Ray telling the man to 'Move it!' and he pushed him back into the house with the gun. Then they were in the house and I couldn't hear or see anything.

"After a while I just got too scared to just sit there in the car, so I got out and snuck up to the house. I still couldn't hear anything in the front so I eased around the house toward the back where the light was on. Just as I got to the back corner of the house the back door opened and Daddy came out. A different old man came out the door behind Daddy, and then Uncle Ray came out holding his rifle to the guy's back. Then the guy I had seen in the front came out and Uncle Tom was following him with his rifle in the man's back. They marched the two old guys out to the barn, which was about a hundred feet from the house, and I just stayed there watching and listening.

"Daddy led the way and walked into the barn. The door was open, and a single light was on somewhere inside, creating enough light for Daddy to step inside and locate a bank of light switches. He began to flip the switches and the inside of the barn was lit up in bright light from several bulbs on the ceiling and along the sides. The barn was pretty much like every large barn I had seen. The front half was open all the way to the roof trusses. Stalls on both sides from the middle to the back of the barn divided the side spaces into squares. A loft ran around the entire barn about fifteen feet above the floor. Bales of hay were stacked on the loft all the way around the barn. More hay was stored in most of the stalls. Daddy pulled the sliding doors of the barn shut, first one side and then the other. When he had closed the doors I ran over to the barn and peeked inside through a window next to the doors. I *heard one of the old men cry out and saw him fall down on his knees.*

"'Get up!' I heard Uncle Ray yell. He grabbed the old man's shirt and roughly pulled him upright. 'Now let's go back to the stall where you two used to take my sister and whip Tom and me.' I noticed that Uncle Tom and Uncle Ray were calling the two old men Lige and Jesse.

"The one called Lige was crying, and he said, 'I don't remember where. It was so long ago.'

"And then Uncle Ray said, 'Then I guess I'll just shoot you here.' He pulled back the hammer on the Winchester. The click of the weapon cocking into firing mode sounded like a hammer on an anvil to me outside, and must have sounded like thunder inside the barn. I remember holding my breath and thinking, 'Please God. Please God. No. No. No. Don't let him shoot.'

"Then I heard the one called Lige say, 'No wait, I remember now.' He got up and sort of stumbled to the last stall on the right side. The one called Jesse followed.

"Using their rifles to prod and direct the two old men, Uncle Ray and Uncle Tom maneuvered them to the fence, standing in the next-to-last stall, facing into the last one. Daddy took some rope from a hook on the wall and pulled his pocket knife from his pocket. He cut pieces of the rope several feet long.

"Uncle Ray told the two, 'Put your hands through the fence, just like you used to make us.'

"When the two old men had stuck their hands through the fence Daddy grabbed them and tied them real tight. I remember the two old men crying out as he jerked the rope tight. Then he looped the rope around the fence so that they couldn't back away. He unbuttoned the shoulder flaps on their overalls and pulled them down below the knees of the two men. Then he took lengths of the rope and tied a loop around their knees, connecting to the fence on both side. The two were tied tight to the stall fence with their overalls down around their ankles. I remember they both had on boxer shorts and their legs were very white. I then saw Daddy going back to the door of the barn and I quickly ran back to the car in front of the house.

"I managed to get back and jump into the front seat just as he came around the side of the house. He stood beside the car and told me to drive it back to the barn. I started it up and drove back there while Daddy walked beside it. He told me to turn around and back up to the side of the barn with the front of the car pointing back toward the road out of there, which I did. Then he opened the trunk again and took out what at first looked like more rope, but as he walked to the side of the car to talk to me I saw that it was a leather bull whip. It was an evil looking thing. Daddy told me to stay in the car and not get out no matter what I heard. I said I would, but as soon as he went back inside and pulled the door shut I jumped out of

156

the car and peeked through a crack where the doors hadn't totally closed.

"The first thing I heard was Uncle Tom saying in a voice I had never heard from him, 'This is the way you used to tie us while you did your business with our sister in that stall. How does it feel?' His voice was real shaky. It sounded like he was going to cry.

"Then Uncle Ray said, 'Tonight the bill comes due for that. You two are going to pay for what you did to our sister, and to us.'

"The two guys were scared to death. The one called Jesse was begging, 'Wait, we're sorry about what happened. We were just kids ourselves. We got some money now. It's all yours if you let us go. We can all just forget this.'

"The only answer he got from Uncle Ray was, 'When hell freezes over,' and he said it so cold I got chills outside the barn.

"When Daddy had come back into the barn they hadn't noticed that he was carrying the coiled up leather whip. But then he flipped it outward, and the whip end jumped out almost ten feet. The two old men saw it and began to cry and fight against the ropes tying them to the stall, but they couldn't get away.

"Uncle Ray said, 'Let me go first. I've been waiting thirty years for this.' He took the whip from Daddy and positioned himself behind the two tied men. He pulled back his arm and flipped the whip behind him, then lashed it forward. I remember thinking that the sound that whip made when it snapped forward was like a snake's hiss. Jesse screamed something awful when the leather tip tore through his underwear and buttocks. Lige began to cry and struggle wildly against his bindings, but he couldn't move away. The whip hissed through the air again and again, leaving angry red streaks on the two tied men from their upper legs to their upper back."

Chapter 27

Starlene paused in her reading. I let out a long breath, discovering that I had been holding it in. No one at the table had said a word since she began. We were all thunderstruck by what we were hearing.

"Jesus Christ!" Billy Rex exclaimed. "I'm almost afraid to hear the rest of this."

"I never had any idea that any of this happened," Robert Earl shuddered.

"I'm afraid of what's coming." Charlie voiced all our fears. "But let's hear it. Keep going Star."

Starlene started to read again. For the briefest instant, I had the feeling that we were not alone, as if I had heard something, or someone in the house, but could not tell what or where it came from. No one else seemed to have noticed it though, so I turned my attention back to Starlene's reading of Son's letter.

"Uncle Ray was whipping them—first one then the other. They were screaming and crying and begging him to stop, but it looked to me like Uncle Ray was sort of out of control. After a little while Daddy and Uncle Tom grabbed him and stopped him. Uncle Ray did not want to stop, but Uncle Tom and Daddy held on to him and told him they had all agreed to take part, to let one of them take a turn. Uncle Tom lashed each of them several times, but not as hard as Uncle Ray did, and then Daddy did it, and he hit them about like Uncle Tom. I mean it was bad, and they kept screaming and begging, but not vicious like with Uncle Ray.

"After a while, when all three had taken a turn, they stopped. From where I was I could see that the backs of the two men were both pretty marked up from their butts to their shoulders. Some of the lash marks were bleeding a little. I remember being surprised that these were two old men. They were both crying and one of them asked if they were going to be released now. Uncle Tom said, 'Hell no! That part was for the times you tied Ray and I to the fence and beat us. Now you are going to pay for assaulting my sister over and over.' One of them asked what they were going to do, and Uncle Ray said, 'We're going to hang your sorry asses.'

"That scared me half to death, and did the same to the Clintons. They started hollering and trying to get loose, but they were tied too well. Daddy and Uncle Tom moved a couple of fifty-five-gallon barrels that were in the back of the barn to a spot under the loft. Uncle Ray had taken some more ropes from inside the barn and made what passed for hangman's nooses. They threw the ropes over a rafter, and moved one of the barrels under each rope.

"I couldn't stay outside any more. I pulled the door open just enough to get inside and said, 'Daddy, please don't do that. I don't want you to kill anyone.'

"Daddy was pretty mad at first. He told me to get back in the car, but I held my ground and just kept saying, 'Please don't. I don't want you to kill anyone.' I was scared to death, but I really didn't want Daddy to kill someone.

"Daddy was really mad at me and kept telling me to get back to the car, but by then I was so scared I couldn't have moved if I wanted to. Finally Uncle Tom came over to where we were standing just inside the barn door.

"'What's going on?' he asked.

"'Son's upset, and doesn't want us to kill them,' Daddy replied angrily.

"'Well Son,' Tom asked, 'do you understand that these men are the Clinton brothers who beat me and your Uncle Ray damned near to death and mistreated your mother horribly?'

"I told him that I understood, but that I did not want my daddy or any of them to kill someone.

"'I want you to be good people,' I pleaded.

"I was crying and shaking, and I think my tears sort of got to Uncle Tom. After a minute or so he took a deep breath and said, 'He's right. I don't want to do it either. I thought I could, but now that we're here, I don't want to do it either.'

"We were standing just inside the door of the barn. Uncle Ray saw us together talking and also walked over. We were far enough away from the Clintons that they could not hear us. We were talking pretty low, and they were hollering anyway. 'What's going on?' Uncle Ray asked, and Daddy explained that Uncle Tom and I did not want to kill them. Uncle Ray was pretty upset at first, but eventually Daddy said he agreed with Uncle Tom and me, that while he had thought he could do it, he realized now that he did not want to go through the rest of his life with a killing on his conscience.

"There was a hell of an argument between the three of them, but finally Uncle Ray calmed down and said, 'Well I'm outvoted three to one. I don't like it, but I'll do whatever the rest of you want to do. What do we do with them now—just leave them tied to the stall?'

"Then Uncle Tom said, 'No. I've got an idea of how to leave this if you will go along with me,' and he explained his idea. We all liked it so that's what we did.

"We looked around the barn till we found some flour sacks we could blind the Clintons with by putting them over their heads. Uncle Tom and Uncle Ray held their rifles on them while Daddy took the ropes tying them to the fence off and then tied their hands behind them. We marched them over to the barrels. They were both *sure they were going to be hung at that point, so they were making a pretty big scene. When we got them to the barrels Uncle Tom made a big deal about putting the nooses over their heads and pulling them snug, and then putting the flour sack over their heads so they were essentially blind. Then we lifted each of them up and stood them on one of the barrels. They were scared to death standing on the barrel with a noose around their neck, and their pants still down around their ankles. When I look back on it now I am amazed one of them did not drop dead from a heart attack.*

"Anyway, Uncle Tom talked real loud, like he was giving instructions to us, saying, 'Tie the ropes off good now, and give them just enough slack to fall off the barrel.' But we didn't tie off the other end of the rope. We just looped it over the rafter and let it hang off the other side. If one of them had fallen while we were there the rope would have slid over and they would have fallen on the ground, but they didn't know that.

"Then Uncle Tom said, 'You don't deserve this, but we are going to give you a chance to live. We are not going to push the barrels over. We are just going to leave. If you can stand up there on those barrels till morning, someone will find you and let you go. If you try to get off and the barrel falls over, you will hang yourself. It's up to you. I hope you fall off and end your miserable lives. If you make it to morning and survive, here's the deal—we have written down in great detail what you boys did to us and our sister. If you ever try to come after any of us that story will go to the law and the newspapers all over the Panhandle. If we never hear of you again, it will go to the grave with the last of us. Do you understand?'

"Both of the Clintons were saying things like, 'we understand,' and 'thank you,' and 'we'll never do anything, we promise.' We just left them babbling and walked out of the barn, got in the car, and drove away. The last I ever saw of the Clintons they were standing on top of those barrels with ropes around their necks, then looped over a rafter untied.

"If you look inside the floor cabinet to the left of the sink in my house, you will see one floorboard with a knot in it. If you stick your finger in the knot, you can pull the board up. There is a burlap sack in the space below that board. The last evidence of that night is in that sack."

Starlene paused in the reading. "There's some more here," she said. "But I think we should check to see if the sack is there before we go on. I haven't looked yet."

"This is getting spookier by the minute," Billy Rex shivered. "Who wants to go check?"

"I'll look," Charlie said, and he rose from his chair and walked to the sink. He kneeled and opened the cabinet to the left of the sink. "There is a board with a knot here, just like he said."

Charlie paused to look back at the rest of us, and then reached in. He made a lifting motion, and we heard a scraping sound as the floorboard came out. He laid the board to the side and reached cautiously into the space beneath the missing board. "There's a sack in here all right," he said as he pulled an old burlap sack from the floor. Holding the top of the sack he rose and walked back to the table.

At the table Charlie paused and looked at the rest of us.

"Open it!" Roy Don exclaimed.

"Yeah. Let's see what's in it," I added.

Charlie grabbed the bottom of the sack, turned it upside down, and shook it. At first, I could not tell what the object that fell from the sack was. For the briefest instant I thought it was a dead snake, stiff in a coiled position. Then I recognized the object I had seen in countless Lash LaRue movies.

"That's a bullwhip," I said as I leaned forward to inspect it. The leather whip was coiled into a circle. Time had frozen it into that position. The leather appeared hard and dry. It was black and cracked with age.

Robert Earl reacted to the object and my identification of it as if it had indeed been a snake, pushing abruptly back from the table and exclaiming, "Oh shit! Oh shit!"

"Oh my God," Billy Rex said slowly, staring at the whip.

Roy Don leaned in and reached for the object. He slowly lifted one side, and the entire whip came up on that side, stiff like a small wheel. He pulled it to a position in front of him and leaned in to inspect it closely. After a few moments he said, "Well, it's a bullwhip all right, and it is very old. It's stiff as a board. Most of the end of it is covered with something black."

"If I had to guess," Charlie said, almost casually, "I'd say that's dried blood. And I have a pretty good guess as to whose blood that might be."

"Oh my God," Billy Rex moaned once more.

There was a heavy silence. I broke the silence, saying, "Read the last of Son's letter, Star. What else did he say?"

All eyes except Starlene's remained fixed on the dried old whip as she spoke for Son again.

"Well, you have probably seen what's in the sack by now, and the questions most of you will come to are whether what we did was wrong, and whether you should tell anyone. Well, here's what I think. If this had been a hundred years earlier and men had done what the Clinton brothers had done, they would have been taken out to the nearest tree and hung by the men in the area. No trial. Just lynched. Vigilante style. And as far as I'm concerned, that's what we did—administered justice, Texas style. And I'm damn glad we did.

"It's a hell of a story though, and I decided the family had a right to know. Most of us have heard about how our parents were abused, and most of us have a lot of anger and even guilt about it. I thought you would like to know that it did not go unpunished. There was more to the story. I hope it helps."

Starlene laid the letter down on the table. "That's the end of the letter." She wiped her eyes with a handkerchief Vernon handed her. The room was silent.

"Damn!" Roy Don snorted.

"Great God oh mighty," Billy Rex added.

"All this time, I thought the Clinton brothers had gotten away with it," I said. "I have to admit that there was a part of me that thought our dads were wussies because they didn't do anything, even though logic told me there was nothing they could do. I was wrong on both counts, or so it seems. Are the rest of you thinking Son was right in his evaluation of what they did?"

"I am," Charlie announced. "And I'm damn proud of them."

"As far as I'm concerned," Star spoke sternly, "my mother was abused and my uncles were beaten, and no one did anything about it. I think those bastards got what they deserved, just thirty years too late."

"I think I have to agree with Star," I said. "Now everyone that had a part in this is dead. I think we should let sleeping dogs lie, so to speak." Once more I thought I heard something—perhaps from the back bedroom—but could not really identify what it was or where it came from. Maybe it was just the old house creaking. Maybe it was just a spooky feeling brought on by the story we had just heard.

Billy Rex asked, "What about the Clinton brothers' families? Do they deserve to know what happened to them?"

"Do you think they want to know? Know that their relatives were rapists?" Robert Earl answered. He had been sitting quietly to that point. "I think I lean to letting it stay a family secret. As Tom said, everyone involved is dead, and letting all this out into the open now would only serve to create hurt in both families—ours and theirs. What good would that do?"

"I have to tell you," Roy Don spoke softly. "Hearing this makes me feel a hell of a lot better about what happened. I've felt awful and angry most of my life about what happened to Mother. I am glad to know it didn't go unpunished."

"It's a hell of a story too, isn't it?" I said. "Too bad we can't tell it. Sometime, I'd like my son to know what his grandfather did. Maybe in another twenty years or so."

"I think it'd be a good idea to keep it as a family legend though, and not have any evidence around in case anyone ever decided to look into it," Robert Earl spoke thoughtfully.

"Good point," Billy Rex replied. "What do we do with Son's letter and the whip?"

"Will leather like that burn?" I asked.

"As old and dried out as it is, I bet it'll burn like cord wood," Vernon answered.

"Well, what do the rest of you think?" I looked around the table at my relatives. "Is anyone opposed to burning the evidence?"

No one voiced any objection. "Well," I started. "What about it? Who wants to do the honors?"

"I'll be damned proud to do it," Charlie replied. He reached to the tabletop and picked up the stiff old bullwhip. He got up and crossed to the fireplace and carefully placed the relic on top of the burning logs. Within seconds the whip ignited. Vernon had been right.

"What about the letter? Should we burn it too?" Starlene gathered all the sheets of the letter and put them back into the envelope.

My cousins began to discuss the pros and cons of burning or keeping the letter. Finally there was consensus that the letter should be burned too, but I had not taken part in this exchange. Charlie asked me, "What do you think Tommy? Are you with us on this part?"

But I was not looking at him or paying attention to the question. I was peering at the back bedroom door and straining to hear something, anything, from there—as if I could will it to be so. I still could not be sure if I had heard something, but I was sure something was not quite right.

I said very loudly, "What do you think? You in the back room. Do you think we should burn the letter?"

"What?" Charlie demanded. He looked from me to the bedroom door and back at me again. "What are you…?"

I held out my hand to silence him, and called again, "What do you think back there? Burn it or not?"

"What the hell are you doing?" Billy Rex asked.

"Are you all right?" Starlene seemed concerned that I had lost my mind.

"Just wait a second," I whispered to them, still motioning with my hand in a way that I hoped conveyed a request to stop and stay silent.

For a moment we heard nothing, and I began to think maybe I was crazy and about to be very embarrassed. Then the handle on the door turned and the door slowly opened. What came through the door next was the longest barrel on a handgun I had ever seen, held by a man dressed in jeans and boots with a well-worn western hat. The gun was an old-style revolver, almost an antique, but looked to have been polished and used. There was no doubt in my mind that it would work. It was the kind of long-barreled revolver I had always seen Wild Bill Hickok wear in western movies, and the bearer also wore a holster from his belt. The man was medium height, gray haired with sharp features, all angles, and very thin. He was followed through the door by a second man similarly dressed, but with somewhat younger, softer features. The second man wore a full beard that was just beginning to gray up. He did not carry a weapon. The two of them followed the very long gun held by the first man into the kitchen.

Everyone was shocked into silence, first by the appearance of the two men, but more than that by the unexpected appearance of the gun.

"What the hell?" Charlie finally broke the silence.

"How did you get in here?" Starlene demanded.

"Now everyone just stay calm," the first man spoke. "Let's don't get all excited." The two men came into the kitchen area, and then stopped, appearing to be unsure about what to do next.

They stared at us. We stared at them. No one said anything for several excruciating minutes.

"You planning on shooting someone with that?" I finally asked the first man, nodding at the long pistol.

"Not if I can keep from it," the man carrying the gun answered. "Everyone just stay calm and sit still while I figure this out."

"I take it you guys are Clintons," I said with a sudden glimpse of insight.

"Yes and no," the gun toting one said. "Our mother was a Clinton, sister to the two you been taking about. They were our uncles."

"You're the ones who dug up Son, aren't you," I said, a statement more than a question.

"Yeah. I'm afraid so."

"Why? Why would you do that?"

"We were looking for that letter you just read," the second, younger man finally spoke. "Our uncles made us promise years ago, before they died, that we'd get that letter when the last of your group died. Your folks told them it was written down that night, and our uncles didn't want the story to get out. They made us promise to come here and find that letter and destroy it so no one would ever know. We had to dig your brother up to see if it was in the coffin with him—go to the grave with him like they said."

"Well why the hell didn't you put him back the way you found him?" Roy Don inquired angrily.

"We planned to," the younger man continued, "but when we got him out and searched the coffin, a bunch of high school kids came out to the graveyard to park and drink beer. We were going to wait them out, but then the police came out there to run off the kids, and we figured we'd better get gone before anyone saw the dug up grave."

"Yeah, we're really sorry about that," the first man said. "We never planned on leaving him unburied. We just wanted to see if the letter was in there with him. When it wasn't we came here to search the house, but then you all started showing up and we hid in the bedroom. We been back there listening."

"How did you get here?" Vernon asked.

"We left our truck in a ravine off the road a little ways back," the gun wielder answered.

"Well, now you know for sure the letter existed," I spoke up. "What do you think of our plan to burn it?"

"I think that's a right good plan," he replied.

"Before we do that," I said, "tell us the rest of the story. What happened to your two uncles? Did they stay on those barrels all night?"

The younger of the two answered, "No. From what we have been able to figure out over the years, sometime before morning Lige either fainted or went to sleep and fell off. He broke his hip when he hit the ground, and he never got over that—was crippled for the rest of his life—but his screaming convinced Jesse that the rope was loose. Jesse managed to get off the barrel without falling, but he caught pneumonia from being out in the barn most of the night. He never got his strength back—he was pretty much an invalid till he died too."

"How do you two feel about that, seeing as how you have the gun?" I asked.

"Well, I sure as hell don't like what happened to them," the gunman shrugged. "But then we always knew they were mean old bastards. We never knew exactly what they did till we heard it tonight, but we figured it was something like that. They told us your folks were just mad at them because of some beatings, but Momma told us about your mother being there, and she told us she had suspicions about what Lige and Jesse did. They were family though, and our Momma loved them even though they were hard old men. We promised them we would try to get the letter to keep it a secret."

"Just one more thing," I added. "Does this end it? Our families have been in sort of a feud for about seventy years. People on both sides were hurt—physically and emotionally—one side then the other. Now you've dug up Son. I guess feud protocol would require us to go dig up someone of yours, or some such. But my daddy carried the hurt of this around with him his whole life. Now that I know the whole story I'm not sure he ever had any peace from it. And I doubt your uncles ever got over it either. There was a lot of anger, hate, and hurt involved. I don't want to keep this up. I'm ready to forgive you guys digging up Son if we can say we put an end to this whole thing."

"As far as I'm concerned—it's over," the man holding the gun responded. "And no one else but us knows about this in our family. We'll keep it that way to make sure it's over."

"What about you guys?" I inquired, indicating Starlene, Roy Don, and Charlie. "Son was your brother. Are you ready to forgive and call this over?"

"I'm tired of being angry and hurt," Starlene said wearily. "I forgive. I never want to think about this again."

"Yeah, I'll go along," Roy Don agreed.

"Me too," Charlie affirmed.

I stepped toward the man with the gun and extended my right hand. "It's over," I declared.

"It's over," the man responded as he put the pistol in its holster and took my hand. He had a strong grip. We shook hands while looking intently into one another's eyes. I shook the second man's hand. Then Charlie, Robert Earl, and Roy Don stepped forward and shook their hands, all of us repeating, "It's over."

"Let's really get this over with," Starlene announced. She rose and went to the fireplace. She placed the envelope containing the letter on top of the burning logs and old leather, and it ignited almost immediately.

Charlie walked to the fireplace to join his sister. He placed an arm around her shoulders. The two of them remained at the fireplace staring at the burning history. I walked over to join them. As I went to the fireplace, all of the other relatives and our intruders did likewise. We stood in a semi-circle at the hearth and silently watched our mutual family history burn.

The intruder with the pistol finally broke the silence. "Well, we'd better get back to our truck and get moving."

"I wouldn't waste any time doing that if I were you," Charlie suggested. "Son had a lot of friends here, and if word got out that you guys dug him up I suspect you'd be very unpopular."

"We're leaving right now. We won't be back," the first man answered, but then he stopped at the door and looked back sadly at Starlene. "We're really sorry about what happened to your mother, ma'am," he added, touching the brim of his hat with his hand, and the two of them left.

Chapter 28

After the two intruders had gone, we stood looking into the fireplace, silent as we watched the leather whip burn to an unrecognizable lump of charcoal. I tried to take stock of my feelings. The first realization was that I felt ashamed. I was ashamed of feelings I had had about my father—of thinking that he had somehow done less than he should have about the abuse he and his siblings had endured. At the same time there was a feeling of pride in what they had done. I might never be able to talk about it, but I already liked knowing about it.

"I have to tell you," Robert Earl declared, "I love it that we have a booger of a skeleton in our family closet."

"I have to tell you that I almost messed my pants when that gun came out of that door! That's the longest damn gun I've ever seen," I shot back.

"Almost? I think I did," Billy Rex added with a relieved sigh.

"How'd you know they were there, Tommy?" Roy Don asked.

"I thought I heard something a couple of times," I answered. "But as much as anything, I just had the feeling we were not alone."

"Funny—I had the same sort of feeling," Charlie remarked. "But I really thought it was the ghost of our fathers and Son in the room."

"Damn," I declared. "This was a crowded little house there for a little while. That gun barrel sucked all the oxygen out of the room when it came around the corner."

We laughed and bantered awhile to relieve the tension. Then I said, "All this time I thought our parents had weenied out—not done anything about the abuse. I've always thought they should have told the police, pressed charges, or something. I guess they just blew right past that."

"Talk about closure," Billy Rex responded.

"Shoot," Charlie said as a big grin spread over his face. "It sort of just makes me feel good all over."

"This is going to take some getting used to," I said. "It's hard to believe Son knew about this all these years, and never said anything. I'm not sure I could have done that."

"I think he saw himself as one of them," Starlene explained. "He *was* one of them. He may have been in our generation in terms of age, but he was more a part of their generation in his heart."

"Did we just commit a crime?" Robert Earl demanded suddenly. "Destroying evidence of what might have been a crime?"

"What evidence?" I retorted. "I haven't seen any evidence."

"Me neither," Roy Don agreed. Everyone agreed that we had never seen anything that would suggest anything illegal had taken place.

"You mentioned that you were at a reading of Son's will, Star," I recalled. "What did he want to do with this place?"

"His instructions were to put it up for sale, get whatever we could, and divide up the money between his nieces and nephews as college money. He left some other things too," she continued. "He left the livestock. He said we should sell the stock and divide the proceeds among the immediate family. And he left his old truck to my daughter and her husband. Charlie gets his old guitar."

"That's right!" Charlie exclaimed. "I almost forgot about that. Where is that thing?"

"It's in the first bedroom, hanging on the wall," Starlene answered, and Charlie got up to go fetch the instrument. He came back shortly carrying a well-used, old guitar. He began to softly tune the instrument.

I walked to the front door and stepped out onto the porch. I moved to the chair farthest from the door and sat down. My cousins followed. Starlene and Vernon sat in the two remaining chairs. Billy Rex and Roy Don carried kitchen chairs onto the porch. Roy Don sat with the back of the chair forward, his legs spread to either side, and leaned cross-armed on the chair back. Charlie and Robert Earl sat on the porch with their legs hanging off. Charlie was still tuning the old guitar. We sat looking across what Son had called Peaceful Valley. The only sound was the plinking of the guitar as Charlie worked to bring it back into tune. We were lost in our thoughts, and mesmerized by the view.

"Star," I announced. "Don't put this place up for sale. I'll buy it. Just get an appraisal, and I'll pay whatever they say it's worth on the market."

"Are you serious?" Charlie asked, looking up at me, pausing in the tuning of the guitar.

"Serious as a heart attack," I declared.

"Oh no," Billy Rex said. "Does this mean you've decided to not go back?"

"Not today anyway," I answered. "This place should stay in the family, and it is exactly the kind of place Kathy has been agitating me to move to. I want some options in case I do decide not to go back."

"I think that'd be great," Roy Don said. "The kids get some college money just like Son wanted, and the place stays in the family. If you do come home and live here that'd just be double good."

"Home," I repeated quietly. I liked the sound of it.

As we sat there on the porch, looking out at the valley, the pager on my belt erupted with shrill beeps. I looked at the screen. The page was coming from the hospital administration office in Austin. I remembered Robert Blake's panicked promise to call when Paul Jordan joined him. I pulled the cell phone from my pocket and sat staring—first at the pager and then the cell phone.

"Anyone you know?" Robert Earl inquired, looking back at me from his perch on the edge of the porch.

"Unfortunately yes," I answered, still staring. I thought for a moment, and then made a decision.

I pulled myself up out of the chair, walked to the steps of the porch and slowly descended. I walked across the ground separating the porch from the windmill and the tank.

"What are you doing Tom?" I heard Billy Rex ask, dread in his voice.

I did not answer. When I was about twenty feet from the tank I made an underhand sweep with my right hand and tossed the pager high in the air. I watched as it reached a peak height of about twenty feet and slowly began to fall. It made a small splash when it landed in the center of the tank, and immediately sunk.

"Tom! No! Don't do that!" Billy Rex pleaded from the porch.

"Oh Lordy!" I heard Robert Earl say hoarsely.

"Nice throw!" Charlie declared.

Then I dialed the office number on the cell phone. I heard a single ring and Robert Blake's voice as he answered. I repeated my previous throw and watched the cell phone tumble through the air—up to a peak, seeming to pause, and then accelerating downward to the surface of the water in the tank, another small splash, and silence. I turned and walked back to the porch, up the steps, over to my empty chair, and sat down, exhaling a deep breath.

No one said anything. Robert Earl continued sitting, swinging his legs back and forth, staring at the ground in front of the porch. Charlie continued working at tuning the old guitar. Billy Rex was leaning forward in his chair, elbows on his knees, his face buried in his hands, mumbling to himself. Starlene sat with a shocked look on her face, her left hand covering her mouth, looking at me as if wondering what stupid thing I would do next. Roy Don sat with his chin resting on his crossed arms on the back of the chair he still straddled, a curious grin on his face.

Several moments of tense silence passed before Vernon finally spoke. "Whoever was on that phone—I take it that was *not* the answer they wanted?"

Robert Earl and Charlie spluttered into laughter.

"No kidding!" Billy Rex said, still shaking his head slowly from side to side, but grinning now.

"I wonder how long one of those phones will work underwater?" Roy Don mused. "What do you reckon whoever was on the line heard as it sunk? Maybe they're still listening."

"Tommy, I can't believe you did that!" Starlene finally exclaimed.

"It's something I should've done a long time ago, Star," I answered. "And I don't know how long those things will work in water, but if it's still working, that damned beeper is going off again right now."

We laughed, thinking of the pager beeping shrilly at the bottom of the tank.

Even Billy Rex chuckled a little. Then, smiling but still shaking his head from side to side, he asked, "Well Tommy, does *this* mean you aren't going back to your job?"

"I don't know, Billy Rex," I replied as I sat back in the chair, resting my head on the back, feeling the tension drain out of me. "It means I'm not ready to go back right now, this afternoon. When you've heard a story like the one we just heard from Son, and looked down the wrong end of a gun barrel, all that stuff back at the hospital just doesn't seem that important any more. I need to think for a while."

"Well, what are you going to do in the meantime?" Billy Rex continued. "Do you think they'll fire you?"

"Well. I think I'll hang around here for a while. Sit on the porch. Look at the view. Try to work some things out," I responded, closing my eyes. "They won't fire me outright though. That would cost them too much money, and create bad publicity. If I were to decide to not go back they would authorize someone on the board to negotiate a resignation from me. I'm actually in a pretty good position here. I could probably negotiate a nice settlement if it came to that."

"Well, could you use some company?" Charlie interjected, stopping his work on the guitar and looking at me. "I think I could use a few days of intense navel contemplation myself. We could stay here, you being the prospective owner and all."

"I think that's a great idea." I opened my eyes and looked over at him. "There's plenty of room. But I thought you were going to play in a golf tournament in Marfa?"

"Ahhhh. Those assholes don't even know who I am, or used to be. They won't mind at all if I don't show up." Charlie gave a brief, embarrassed smile, and then he went back to tuning the guitar.

"Well, I'd better get on the road before I decide to go AWOL too," Billy Rex said as he rose from his chair, stretching. "I've got a long way to go."

He walked down the stairs off the porch, stopped, and turned back to me. "Do you want me to call Kathy when I get home Tommy? What should I tell her?"

"Naahhh," I said. "I'll call her. She'll be thrilled. This place is what she has always dreamed about. She'll probably want me to make an offer on the horse too."

"I'm jealous as hell," Billy Rex announced. "I'd like to stay too. If you guys are still here next weekend I'm going to drive back to check on you."

"I've got to go too," Roy Don said as he rose up from the chair he was straddling. "It's a long way to San Antonio. I'll see all of you at Thanksgiving."

"Me too," Robert Earl said. "I'd better get going, but I will definitely be back."

After handshakes and hugs all around, Billy Rex, Robert Earl, and Roy Don walked down the steps of the porch and around to where their cars were parked. We heard doors shutting and engines starting, and the sound of tires crunching on earth and rocks as they drove away. Then there was no sound.

"We've got to meet the kids after church," Starlene said, rising from her chair. Vernon also got up, and the two of them descended the steps. "Why don't the two of you come over to our place for supper tonight? About six?"

I had leaned back in my chair, unable to keep my eyes open. I did not answer, but I heard Charlie say, "I'll bring him over." The sounds of Starlene and Vernon leaving drifted around me. I was minimally aware that Charlie finished tuning the guitar and began strumming and singing softly. I barely heard. I was lost in the sounds of the windmill blades creaking contentedly as they turned, and the soft chatter of water trickling into the tank. I was six years old again, listening to the sounds of the windmill drifting in through my open bedroom window on a soft summer night. I was home. Then I was asleep, and I slept a more peaceful sleep than I had in years.

"My heroes have always been cowboys,
And they still are it seems.
Always in search of,
And one step in back of
Themselves and their slow moving dreams."

About the Author

Tom Hardy is a native Texan, the son of a father who left home at thirteen to become a working cowboy and a mother of Cherokee lineage. He was born and raised in Fort Stockton and Alpine in far West Texas. He attended Sam Houston State University on an athletic scholarship and majored in business administration. After ten years as a teacher and coach at the high school and college levels, he returned to school and received a master's degree in health care administration from Trinity University in San Antonio and moved into hospital administration.

As he was making the transition to health care, he wrote his first novel, *Unsportsmanlike Conduct*, an unflattering view of college football, published in 1983. He and his wife Patricia have raised three children. Retirement from the corporate world has allowed him time to return to writing. *Slow Moving Dreams* is his second novel, and he is working on his third. All of his books are set in West Texas where he was raised and continues to enjoy a love of the land and people who make West Texas special.